The Ninety-Ninth Bride

BY CATHERINE FARIS KING

Copyright Information

Copyright © 2022 Catherine Faris King Cover Illustration by Reiko Murakami
Paperback book design by Thea James

Contents

Prologue

These are but a few of the races that inhabit our wrinkled world.

This is how God made the mermaids: God lobbed a spitball into the ocean, and willed that mermaids should be, and should be custodians of all the waters He had made, but bound within those waters.

This is how God made the djinn: God took six drops of his own blood, and willed that djinn should sprout from these, and be creatures of fire. Further, they should be bound by the number six, and be custodians of magic and justice, but bound to the things of this world.

This is how God made the nasnas: God took a toenail clipping and halved it, and willed that nasnas should be, half people yet stern and strong, and that they should be custodians of the ways to the underworld, but always they should search for completion, first in this world, and then with God.

This is how God made humankind: God took the clotted blood from His wound, and mixed it with earth, and willed that humans should be truly in His image, and custodians of all the world, responsible and willing.

Part One

The Bride

Perhaps you have heard tell of a wise girl named Scheherazade. She was a clever student who listened to the talk of the scholars, the servants, and the stars. She was unlucky enough to live in an evil time, under the rule of a wild man. The Sultan of her Kingdom was driven mad over the betrayal of his wife. Scheherazade offered to become the King's new bride. The King intended to kill her, as he had killed all his previous wives, but Scheherazade's courage was undaunted and her wits were without limit. Instead of being his wife, she told him one thousand and one stories, each more dazzling than the one before, so enthralling that the King could not bear to kill her without hearing its ending — which always lurked in the night to come. By telling stories, Scheherazade kept her life, healed the King's madness, and saved her Kingdom.

Oh, yes…perhaps you have heard tell that she had a sister. She was named Dunyazhade. Less clever, less beautiful, and less brave, her main purpose was to listen to the stories that Scheherazade told.

Perhaps you have not heard the whole story.

Once upon a time, in Arabia, a girl was born in a city called Al-Rayyan. While the people celebrated and feasted, her mother struggled to bring her into the world.

The child was born at midnight. "It's a girl," said the exhausted midwife. "Do you have a name for her?" The mother nodded, sweat clinging to her ashen brow. "Dunya," she said, and held out her arms.

The midwife gave Dunya to her mother. She pitied the young woman, who sounded like she was exhausted beyond endurance. The mother kept talking, rambling. "No. I have to live. I'll fight for her. I'll give her a place in her father's household…will you take care of her? I'd rather…but that will do. Do you promise? Good. Thank you."

"Dunya—that name means 'the world,' doesn't it?" asked the midwife. She turned from the mother and her child and poured water from an ewer to wash her hands, and thought the mother was a bit rude for not answering.
Then, when her hands were dry, she turned around and saw.

She regretted her impatience and gently took the little baby from the arms of Death. It wasn't the first time she had undertaken this duty.

"Don't worry, Dunya," she said to the little one. "Many live without mothers and get by fine. And your father is a mighty man. You'll have a good place."

When the midwife told Dunya's father of her mother's death, he laid a hand over his eyes and sighed deeply.

"I'm too old for this," he said.

Just a wall away, Al-Rayyan celebrated with all of its people—some of whom were even human. In the Generous City, djinn blew out enormous smoke rings on the rooftops, and mermaids surfaced in the torch-lit canals. Still, Death took away its share of souls that night, as on all nights. It was the Feast of the Sacrifice.

"I'm too old for this," Shareef had said, and he put his newest daughter in the care of his mother, apparently not thinking that she was too old for any of this.

At first, Grandmother Aaliya did not like having another child to look after. She had done her share of that labor! And she had earned her rest, she said to anyone who would listen. But of Shareef's three wives, they were each absorbed with their own children and their own affairs, and Shareef, the Grand Vizier of the Kingdom, blocked his ears to his mother's reasoning. Eventually, Grandmother Aaliya grew tired of complaining. And the baby still needed looking after. Besides, what were servants for?

And so, Dunya grew up in her grandmother's quarters. She knew of the rest of her family, but they dwelled on the other side of the household, in a busier home. Dunya's world was limited to Grandmother's quarters and servants, livened by visits to Grandmother's elderly friends.

"Children should be seen, not heard," her grandmother told her, gently but firmly. And so Dunya, on these visits, had nothing to do but listen.

She didn't understand most of the stories shared by Grandmother and her friends, but she knew they all had to do with people who were dead now. That lent them an eerie, almost sacred quality. They needed her full attention, even if she didn't understand.

It was a quiet life, with many rules to obey, and much to learn.

When Dunya was thirteen, the announcement rang out across the Kingdom: the Sultan was to be wed.

This meant a feast for all the people, common and noble; it meant a chance to make merry and celebrate; it meant that officers would return from the border skirmishes. It also meant gifts aplenty for the Sultan and new Sultana. And no one had to make a greater gift than the Grand Vizier.

On this special occasion, Shareef and his first wife paid a visit to Grandmother Aaliya, to ask her for advice on the matter.

"You shouldn't have to shower him with gifts," was Aaliya's first remark. "You already offer your best counsel and loyalty. That should outweigh all the perfumes and dyes of the world."

"They should, but alas, they do not," said Shareef. "Our Sultan is rather picky. He likes his shows of respect to be elaborate and frequent. I would like to impress him, without bankrupting our household."

"This is a wedding, isn't it?" Aaliya asked. "Perhaps focus on what his bride might enjoy. Maybe one of your girls, offered in service to the Sultana. Dunya would make an excellent lady-in-waiting."

"Dunya?" said First Wife Noora. "But she's too…" she glanced at Dunya and swallowed whatever she would say next.

"The girl is obedient, quiet, eager to please, and quite clever," said Aaliya. "And it would put her in the eye of the court. She might marry well."

"Please, Mother, be sensible," said Shareef. "Just look at her! She's fragile, like her mother. She won't live to see her wedding day." He rolled his eyes when his mother and first wife spat against evil. "But you are right, about the Sultana. She's very beautiful. I saw her portrait myself. Beautiful women are always vain. I shall buy a mirror for her, from the farthest country I can think of." He turned abruptly, leaving the women behind. "Thank you, Mother."

"Don't let me detain you," said Aaliya, drily.

When they left, Aaliya turned to what looked like a perfectly innocent curtain hanging against the wall. "Dunya! I know you are eavesdropping. Come out. I'm not mad."

Dunya crept out from behind the curtain. "Grandmother?" she said.

"Don't be afraid; eavesdropping is an ancient tradition in my family. What is it?"

"Am I really…" Dunya paused. "Will I truly not live to see my wedding day?"

Grandmother clucked her tongue. "My son always imagines the worst. It makes him a good Vizier, but it is very bad for the family. You'll live a long time, my dear. I shall speak to Death on your behalf. Come here and give your Sittou a hug."

Dunya hurried over and hugged her. Grandmother smelled like rosewater and tea. "You are going to live for a very long time," Grandmother said again.

"Grandmother…" Dunya stared up at her grandmother with wide dark eyes.

"What now?"

"The Sultan loves the woman he's marrying, right?" When Grandmother didn't answer, Dunya went on, "He

must, if she's so beautiful and well-bred, like Father says."

"Or he married her for a bit of land, or a good opportunity to expand the business of the Kingdom. Marriages like that are another ancient tradition of our family. It's why I married my husband. It's why your mother married your father…."

But Dunya had heard enough. She slipped out of Grandmother's arms and went to her own room. So that was the story of how she came to be! A marriage for a bit of land. Or for business opportunity. It seemed to Dunya, lying in bed and, for once, ignoring her grandmother's calling voice, that she had a very small, measured life ahead of her, if her origin was as mean as all that.

Grandmother came into Dunya's room and stroked the girl's dark hair, promising Dunya vaguely that she would be sure to marry well, and not to be sad, and Grandmother Aaliya was getting too old for all this.

Dunya's father invited a merchant of glass and mirrors into his home. All of the sons were welcomed to come and admire the merchant's wares. The two elder daughters, along with Shareef's wives, watched the proceedings from behind a screen, and whispered to intermediaries when they wished to purchase anything. The younger daughters, including Dunya, were allowed to examine the stall at arm's length.

While her brothers grabbed at pieces of glass, and wondered what they could get their father to purchase, Dunya hung back. She watched the merchant, a flighty and expressive man. He had come from outside the walls of her father's estate. What was his life? What did he see, know, experience out there in the city?

Right now, the merchant was talking of his fine mirrors. "You see, long ago a djinni fell in love with a merry sand spirit. They danced together, they embraced, they made a garden of perfect glass out in the desert wastes. But, alas, the sand spirit perished in a windstorm, and the djinni wandered the wide deserts of Africa, looking for her love. But she found her way into a glassworks, where a cunning glazier— my grandfather!—mprisoned her within a little amulet. She provides the fire for our glassworks. So you see, every one of these pieces is infused with magic and mystery."

"A djinni?" asked Dunya's second oldest brother. "This isn't a nursery tale. Treat us like adults, please."

The merchant gave a little bow and stroked his beard with his hand.

How strange, Dunya suddenly realized that everything she'd seen him do today had been done only with his right hand. And he had a left hand, but it flickered, now that she looked at it, like a shadow. And the left side of his face seemed to drag. Dunya remembered that her grandmother had warned about this. It was a stroke; it happened sometimes to the elderly or the very stressed.

Dunya did not want to draw attention to herself, but she could not sit idly by if the man truly was in danger. She approached him, laying a hand upon his left arm.

"Sir," she asked, "Pardon my rudeness, but are you feeling quite well?"

He looked at her, and his eye gleamed piercingly— his right eye, Dunya noticed. "Why do you ask?"

"You haven't lifted your left hand since entering the house. And your face lists to the side..."

To her surprise, he smiled. They were standing far enough away from the crowd that no one could overhear them.

"You see very clearly," he said. He pointed to his cart. "Do you see anything odd in those reflections?"

Dunya turned, her gaze sweeping across the various mirrors in search of something amiss. But in each of their surfaces, the merchant's reflection appeared just as he did in her eyes. "No, nothing odd," she replied, and turned back to him.

He had pulled out a small glass in a metal case. "This," he said to her in a very low voice, "is more valuable than all the other mirrors I have, put together." "Truly?" Dunya asked.

He smiled again, and gave a little shrug. "Well, close enough." He tilted it so that she could see his reflection. "Now what do you see?"

Dunya stifled a gasp. In the mirror, the merchant appeared as only half of a person, as though he had been cleanly cut down the middle. One eye looked at her, half a mouth smiled at her. Where he was cut, rough stone gleamed back at her.

Dunya looked up at him, and now she could see that his left half was sort of stitched onto his true self, an illusion, like a cloudbank.

"You're—" she stumbled, remembering the creature but not the name, "you're a half…half-man? A nasnas," she remembered at last.

The man nodded. "You have the way of seeing true. It's a rare gift. Cultivate it."

"I've never seen a half-person before," Dunya said.

The man frowned. "More people are halved than you may think, little one. Broken down the middle, searching for wholeness. I myself prefer the term nasnas."

"I apologize for my rudeness." Dunya exclaimed, bowing quickly.

"Dunya!" cried her father, having caught just this last exchange. "Are you bothering our guest?"

"Not in the least, sire," said the merchant. He caught Dunya's eye again. This time, she dared to ask a question.

"The story about the djinni, sir…was it true?"

He shrugged and gave her a wink with his right eye. "Let's say it was half true."

In the end, the merchant sold no djinni-blown glass. Instead he sold a huge, circular mirror from Venice, the city on water, to Dunya's father, and the Vizier indicated that that was sufficient expense for the day. The merchant packed up his wares and left the home without incident, except to look back at Dunya as he departed and tap his right eye knowingly. The day was over.

It occurred to Dunya later that evening that perhaps a more appropriate reaction at that time would have been to say something like, But nasnas are only a story, or to reject the existence of nasnas immediately and shriek that the merchant was a liar, an imposter, a thief who wanted to swindle them out of their money. But she had instead been very phlegmatic from the first observation, and, she decided that her reaction had been a good one.

It was the Sultan's wedding day.

Shareef outfitted his family with great expense and great pride, and led the procession to the Palace. Dunya, outfitted with somewhat less expense than her sisters, nevertheless liked her new outfit all of springtime green and her eyes were wide with wonder as she entered the Palace for the first time.

The Palace took Dunya's breath away. Banners and flags crisscrossed the sky; the walls were the speckled color of eggshells, interrupted by carnelian. On the ground, there were fountains and gardens laid out so perfectly they must have mirrored Paradise—all fed, according to Dunya's father, by a special cistern below the Palace itself. Its domed towers glowed in the sunset light, and there was a rumor of fireworks after nightfall.

As the Vizier's family processed through the courtyard— with Dunya, of course, taking the last place—they could glimpse other parts of the festivities. There was the ambassador's courtyard, and a pavilion set up for the lesser nobility. Dunya's older sister tarried to get a better look at the jugglers and tumblers rehearsing.

The Vizier's second wife chided her daughter for her immodesty. Dunya also tarried a moment, but no one chided her. She started to pay more attention to the route that they took.

When they passed a room full of books and scrolls, Dunya felt the needling voice of temptation and, since there was no one to stop her, gave in at once--she slipped away. The Vizier's family would dine with the Sultan himself and the very highest nobility in the land. So that room would be easy enough to find, right?

Gold glittered in three different alphabets on a hundred different spines. Dunya ambled down the corridor between books, and took a turn here, and a turn there, content for now simply to read the spines. The books' subjects ranged from a dissertation on the human eye, to the engineering of the Venetian canals, to the composition of soil in China. There was so much to learn! Dunya felt dwarfed, awestruck by how much there was to know, especially compared to her small knowledge, the little world she lived in. But something in her railed against this overwhelmed feeling. Why should I know so little? She thought, frustrated. Why should I almost never get to leave my father's house?

She took another turn, then looked back. She suddenly realized she wasn't sure how to get back to her family.

That was bad.

She turned back and tried to retrace her steps. At first the books helped her—there was the section about botany, there was the section about theology—but eventually her steps faltered, and she came to a star-shaped intersection and didn't remember at all where her eyes or feet had been.

She heard footsteps nearby. Oh, no. As if this couldn't get worse. She was going to be caught and punished, no doubt.

She tried to duck behind a shelf, but instead of an alcove, she found she was in a larger, more open gallery— and there was a strange young man, rather close, and Dunya wanted to die.

"What are you doing here?" he asked.

"Nothing. I'm no one," she said, trying to find a way out, trying to hide her face, trying to be modest, for the love of God.

"I won't hurt you," said the man.

Dunya stopped trying to shy away, and looked up—and up. The man was very tall, and a little older than her. He was dressed, she saw, for hard horseback riding, and looked quite tired. He held a book in one hand.

"Are you lost?" he asked.

She nodded. "I'm here for the wedding," she stammered, feeling some explanation was needed.

He nodded. "I figured. What is your family?"

"My father is Shareef, the Grand Vizier."

The man lifted his eyebrows. "I didn't know old Shareef had any daughters your age," he replied. "I'm Munir. You must have a name," he prompted.

She gave a rushed bow. "Dunya. Dunya is my name."

"We should return you to your father," said Munir, to Dunya's great relief. "But first, I must return this book…It's had an adventurous three months!" he said, half to himself, as he turned to scan the bookshelves. "Let me see…yes, it went just here. Very good. Now I can get ready. But first, you are my guest, and I must take care of you."

"I'm not your guest," Dunya said. She didn't like to speak, but she had to correct him. "You just happened to find me."

Now the man smiled at her, with some surprise. "We wedding guests must look out for one another."

"There you are!" came a man's voice from the other end of the gallery. Dunya flinched, but it was Munir who turned.

"Ah. Hussein. Were you looking for me? I told everyone I would return the book first."

"You're not even dressed yet!" said Hussein. He was an athletic-looking man, dressed elegantly, but there was a shine and disarray about him that suggested he had only barely washed up and threw some clothes on. "We cannot enter the hall without you! And who is this? A girl from the harem?"

"I should think not," said Munir. Dunya hid a giggle with her hand. The harem? Did she look like a courtesan? Or a royal aunt? Munir went on. "She's a daughter of the Vizier. Show her some respect."

Hussein made a creditable bow. "My lady." He glanced up at Munir. "I shouldn't have to warn you about the Sultan's temper, your Highness."

"And you don't need to insult my intelligence by doing so," said Munir. "He won't kill me for being a few more minutes late."

"Are you sure?" Hussein muttered, but Munir had turned back to Dunya.

"Who are you, to the Sultan?" Dunya asked him. He must belong to the Palace—this library was his to use.
That's why he knew the books like old friends.

"I am the son of the late Vizier Junayd, and a cousin of the Sultan's, some two or three times removed…and we were playmates," he added. "Years ago."

"Was it necessary to add that?" Hussein asked him.

"The lady asked," Munir said, "and remember your rank; we are not in camp anymore. Now, to you, young lady. Shall I send you back with a servant? How would your father react to that?" There was a pause.

Dunya realized he was waiting for her to answer. "You can't be asking me, sire—sir…"

"I am asking you. And don't worry about my title."

"My father would be ashamed of my impropriety, I think," Dunya's replied. "But no one misses me, I'm sure."

"Oh, someone must," said Munir, waving his hand. "Do you mind waiting a few more minutes?"

"No. Why?"

"I have an idea."

Dunya followed Munir and Hussein to Munir's quarters. There was a woman waiting by the door. Her hair was silver and her gaze slightly amused, and Munir called out when he saw her.

"Morgiana!" he exclaimed. He hugged her and said, "You're just the person I wanted to see."

"Oh, you wanted to welcome your old auntie as soon as you came back from the border?" she asked, with a smile.

"No—I wanted you to serve as a chaperone. There's a little girl here whose reputation is in serious danger."

"Oh, very funny," Morgiana replied, pinching the tall man's cheek. "I feel very appreciated."

"I'm sorry, Morgiana, but I'm already late. I'll have to visit you later."

"Be sure you do. I've missed you greatly, my boy." She nodded at Hussein, "I've read good things about you in my

Lord's letters. You are a good Captain." Hussein actually

blushed.

"Morgiana, if you could do me a favor, I need to get ready for my Lord's wedding party..." Munir sighed. "Could you please look after Shareef's daughter for me?"

"It would be my pleasure," said Morgiana. When Munir disappeared into his rooms, Morgiana looked at Dunya, who had been standing silently, observing the entire exchange. Dunya's head was spinning with all of these new people to know. Perhaps Morgiana could infer that from the expression on her face, because she simply asked if Dunya could play chess.

Dunya said no, but that she was willing to learn.

She had only just gotten as far as the movement of the war elephants when Munir re-emerged, dressed in deep blue robes, looking somewhat refreshed, though still weary. He also, Dunya realized, was rather handsome, in a stretchedout sort of way. She felt silly for having not noticed earlier. She tried to swallow and clear her throat, but her ability to talk seemed to have left her entirely.

Fortunately, she did not need to talk. Munir's cheer had deserted him along with his riding gear, and he barely spared the women a glance as he called up his men—a small company of cavalry officers—nd asked for Morgiana and Dunya to walk directly behind him. For the second time that day, Dunya was in a procession, but this time, she was nearly at its head.

Munir led the way, his steps never faltering as he made his way through the very heart of the Palace, to a great courtyard where flowers spilled down over the walls and hundreds of courtiers and diplomats chattered over plates of food and drink. A hush fell over the crowd when Munir and his company arrived in their midst.

There was a great table at one end of the courtyard, where Dunya spotted her father, beside the Sultan and his wife. The procession made its way to the head table, marching around the grand fountain at the center of the banquet. Dunya eyed her family nervously, stealing glances but then looking away at the ground when she saw the looks of shock on their faces. She made a kind of squeaking noise, horrified at what they must think—

"Show no fear," said Morgiana. "Be as scared as you like, but these hyenas will pounce on weakness." When Dunya looked up at her, Morgiana winked.

Now Munir and his entourage stood before the head table. And Munir spoke, addressing himself to the Grand Vizier.

"Vizier Shareef, there was a strayed member of your party." Munir held his hand out towards Dunya, and she approached and made the deepest bow that she could. She didn't dare look at her father's face. "I found her in the library, seeking out the wisdom of the ages. It is a thirst you would do well to slake." Dunya glanced up at him, and he smiled at her. Her pulse quickened.

"You pay your respects to the Vizier before you greet me?" came another voice—a man's voice, but seething with anger.

"My Lord," said Munir, "I meant no disrespect."

Everyone bowed, except for Dunya. She was a minute late, and she saw who spoke—it was the Sultan.

"You meant no disrespect? Somehow I doubt that."

"This young lady is my guest," Munir continued. "I must treat her honorably."

Dunya prayed that she would be left out of this.

"She is my guest, and I am your host," said the Sultan. "You should have honored me first."

And then Dunya heard a new voice: "Darling, be at peace. Your cousin just made a little mistake, I'm sure. How many miles did you ride today, Munir?"

Dunya dared to look up now. The speaker was the Sultana, wearing silver robes embroidered with the moon. She looked like no one that Dunya had ever seen before – her hair fell in a yellow sheet past her waist, and her skin was pale as jasmine petals. But her smile was beautiful, and she smiled at Dunya as Munir spoke.

"We set out at first light today, and just reached the Palace," said Munir. "It has been a five day ride. I wanted to return a book to the library, and there I found her."

"There, you see, husband?" the Sultana asked. "He must be tired. And all his intentions are good. It's our wedding night. Shall we drop this little quarrel?"

The Sultan turned to her and smiled reluctantly. "Fine. Nothing but goodwill on this night. You can sit beside your father," he said, gesturing at Dunya. She recognized this as a dismissal, and hurried to sit beside her father, bowing every other step or so.

Shareef, sitting beside the Sultan, looked furious, but the Sultana smiled across her husband at Dunya. It was a conspiratorial grin, the kind that said, I'm so glad you're

here, it was so boring until you arrived.

And so, Dunya found herself eating at the high table, with a fine view of the best of the wedding proceedings. She was on her very best manners for the entire evening, and her father had no more reason to be ashamed of her. After a while he nearly forgot her, as she knew he would.

Dunya took a chance to observe all the people around her. The Sultana spoke only to her new husband; Munir kept sneaking glances over at Dunya, and at the Sultana.

The first gifts to be presented came from the Sultana's family, as part of her dowry. Her father explained the gifts in accented Arabic, and attendants scurried to and fro, bringing one gift after another. All of them were dressed in the strange costumes of the far North.

The gifts included fine saddles and weapons, and Dunya saw her father frown—he didn't like the prospect of war, she thought.

It was the final gift that made Dunya gasp—a huge clay pot, and in the pot grew a small tree. Everyone fell silent at the sight—or rather, the sound. Every leaf had a tiny face growing on it, and each leaf sang softly, so the leaves, as they shifted, created a beautiful chorus.

"The Singing Tree," explained the Sultana's father, "is the jewel in the crown of our realm. This sapling, this magic made tame, will show our esteem for Al-Rayyan, and our hope for this union."

The guests applauded and the Sultan rose to his feet to express heartfelt thanks. The Sultana, Dunya noticed, kept bright eyes on the tree, until it was taken out of sight.

Next, dinner was served. As the company ate, more ambassadors came before the Sultan and presented their gifts. Dunya enjoyed watching them, not that they were meant for her, but it gave her a sense of being connected to the wide world, to see people who had come from so far away. There was a general from Ethiopia; there was a scholar from China; there was a prince from India. All presented dazzling gifts—a squadron of soldiers, a jade statue of a dragon, an encyclopedia of medicine—and at some point Dunya saw Morgiana slipping away, out the back of the courtyard.

She must be returning to the Palace harem, Dunya thought. It was a lonely life for the women there——some of them had barely any status outside of the harem walls. There lived some future consorts of the Sultan, and some older members of the nobility, waiting out their days. She shook her head, and her first thought was that the possible influence would not be worth the isolation. Then she looked at her father, and the way he steadfastly avoided making eye contact with her, and she reconsidered…

The Sultan stood up abruptly, and all the men in the courtyard immediately got to their feet. He nodded at them and then departed, his gold and red robes fluttering behind him.

"Shareef," said the Sultana, who had lingered at the table. "I would like to talk to your daughter." Her voice was musical and strangely accented.

This took him completely by surprise, but he gestured quickly to Dunya. "Well, then, go on!" he snapped at his daughter.

Dunya obeyed, and went to the Sultana. She smiled at Dunya, and it was a smile like that of a rose—curled up tight and promising secrets. "Are you enjoying yourself?" she asked.

"I am. Thank you for asking," Dunya replied. The Sultana's beauty was dazzling, and Dunya couldn't hold onto her thoughts, except the idea that she must not let her family down.

"You were exploring the library?" the Sultana asked. Dunya nodded. "I hear it's a wonderful archive."

"It is!" Dunya replied. "But I only got to see the tiniest part of it."

"Perhaps, a little later, I can invite you over and show you more of it," said the Sultana. "Would you like that?"

Dunya nodded eagerly, just as the wave of men standing up told her the Sultan had returned.

"Until we meet in the library, then," said the Sultana, and Dunya went back to her seat.

She could barely see the stars for all the lanterns in the courtyard, but she also had the best view for the fireworks.

It was a good night.

The Mad Sultan

Dunya's grandmother died shortly after the Sultan's wedding.

A month prior, First Wife Noora had declared that Grandmother Aaliya was too weak to attend the festivities. Grandmother had spent the entire month complaining that this was unjust. It was disrespectful of her age, and wasn't she the premier woman of the house? The day that Grandmother abruptly stopped complaining was the day that Dunya had to hurry to find First Wife Noora to inform her that Grandmother had fallen ill.

Dunya tried to be a patient and good nurse to her grandmother, but her fear ate at her, making her clumsy and more awkward than usual, especially around her older sisters as they chattered and went about their chores as if the world wasn't ending. One day, Dunya snapped, telling her older sisters to be quiet, for God's sake, because Grandmother would be dead soon.

First Wife Noora scolded Dunya in front of the entire family for her thoughtlessness. Dunya never knew that Noora and the other wives had to laugh about it later that evening, or else they would have all cried—Dunya had to spend the rest of the day in bed sobbing, burning with mortification and the belief that she'd somehow sped up her grandmother's demise by voicing the unthinkable.

But Grandmother would be dead soon. Dunya had seen many of Grandmother's friends pass away over the years, one at a time. Their voices were silenced, their houses were closed up, and Grandmother stopped mentioning their names because they made her cry. There was no point, as Dunya saw it, in dancing around the fact.

Grandmother Aaliyah called Dunya to her the next day.

"I'm sorry, Sittou," said Dunya.

"You think you're the only one with something to be sorry for?" Grandmother asked. "Come here. Take my hand." Dunya slipped her hand into her grandmother's, which was quite cold. "I am sorry that I told you to be so quiet. I'm sorry I didn't tell you more things about your mother. She was a good woman. Rashida was her name. There is a plot of land—an olive grove, I believe—and it belongs only to your mother's bloodline." The old woman smiled at her grandchild, wrinkles in the corners of her eyes. "It belongs to you now, and I hope you visit it someday." Dunya was quiet.

"You're not getting sentimental now?"

"I don't have anyone in the world but you," said Dunya. "I'm selfish, I know, but I don't want to be alone."

"You won't be alone," said Grandmother. "God and His angels are all around, working in mysterious ways..." Her voice grew distant and hazy.

"Sittou, I don't want you to die."

"Do not be afraid. To me, Death is as an old friend. Death comes for all, the high-born and the meekest mouse…you, too, will meet Death, whatever station you find in life."

"I have no station. I have no place, Sittou."

"You will find one. You will grow to meet whatever is demanded of you. I have faith in you, Dunya…Rashida?"

As Grandmother began to call for people who weren't there, Dunya called for the people who were—her father, First Wife Noora, anyone who would listen.

Grandmother died well, surrounded by family, sleeping, and at peace.

And as for Dunya, what she feared came to pass. Without Grandmother to look out for her, she fell into the cracks of the household. First Wife Noora moved into Grandmother's quarters, and Dunya moved into another room, then another. She had no place any longer, if indeed she'd ever had one.

While her family was sequestered in mourning, a message came from the Sultan. The messenger recited familiar words of condolences for the family—and then he asked for Dunya, by name. To Dunya, he handed a slim book.

"A volume of poetry, from the Sultana's hand," he said, "with her good wishes. She asks that you return it within the fortnight."

"T-thank you," Dunya stammered. She stared at the book in her hands. Even with the eyes of her family heavy on her, she couldn't stop smiling.

One Feast of the Sacrifice passed, and then another. Two years passed slowly, and Dunya watched her sisters get married off and move away to their new husbands and homes. Dunya half-heartedly wondered when it would be her turn, if she would ever have a turn. Her oldest two brothers married, and their wives entered the household, and they were happy to boss Dunya around, just as their husbands did—there was always at least one person below them in the family pecking order.

The books that the Sultana sent were Dunya's best consolation. She returned them with her father or by Palace messenger. Notes—small, very polite, but enthusiastic on Dunya's part—passed with the books. She did not see the Sultana in person again, but cherished a hope that, someday, she might.

She never did get to visit the olive grove. She was too shy to ask her father to take her.

Dunya was sitting up one night—not reading, but thinking. Her sixteenth birthday was approaching. It was past midnight when she heard the sound of beating hooves – her father's gelding. Servants hurried to greet him properly. But why was he home so late? Dunya went to investigate. She slipped into the room where he slurped at passionfruit sharbat and rubbed his forehead, ignoring the anxious family around him. Second Wife Amira asked him what was wrong.

He looked at her and said, in a low voice that carried through the room, "The Sultana is dead."

First Wife Noora gasped. Into Dunya's vision flashed the most recent gift from the Sultana, a prayer book with vivid illuminations. Dunya's heart seemed to turn empty in her chest—the Sultana would never see those paintings again. The jasmine-pale woman with her kind notes and—Dunya pressed cold fingers into her forehead. This couldn't be. She would never see that rose-like smile again. Dunya wanted to ask how, but her father's look forbade it.

Dunya returned to the chamber she shared with two sisters—but she didn't think she would sleep. She went through the collection of notes from the Sultana—there was a unique message to go with each book.

"Of all these tales, I like the tale of Saturn the best," said one note.

"I try to copy this calligraphy, but my form is poor. Maybe you'll have better luck," said another.

"Look at the illustration on page twenty-one. What a sweet child!" That one brought the tears. The idea pressed on Dunya's mind—the Sultana had died in childbirth, perhaps bringing to the world a child she'd wanted and loved.

When Dunya began to cry, she could not stop. The hand that wrote these notes was stilled forever –and –

"Dunya, go to bed already, it's almost morning," said one of her sisters.

Dunya crawled into bed, and stifled her weeping as best she could. It wasn't fair. It wasn't fair. How could this happen?

The next day, the Vizier's family wore black to mourn the poor woman. But, oddly, there were no citywide showings of grief, as befitted a deceased Sultana. If Dunya stretched her memory, she could remember the death of the Sultan's mother—that had merited a day of mourning, and a procession over the main streets and bridges of AlRayyan.

The second day after the news came, Dunya approached her father and said, "I want to return the book that the Sultana loaned me."

Her father looked at her and shook his head. "Consider the book yours. I would not return it to the Sultan now for the world."

"But it belongs to the Palace. Perhaps, during her funeral –" Her father waved her away, but Dunya persisted, "Father, when is the funeral?"

"The woman is buried already," her father snapped, "and if you love your life, don't speak that woman's name out loud—ever."

"But–"

"Not another word! Do not bother to arrive for supper tonight," he added, and his eyes flashed.

Dunya bowed her head and left, but she quietly seethed. She was almost sixteen, practically a woman, and her father was wrong to treat her like a child. But he was in a mood, and his wives would side with him.

That night, Dunya snuck out of her bedroom into the kitchen, intending to find food. But while she was crossing the courtyard, she heard noises. She found a hiding spot, crouched among the birds of paradise and palm fronds in one corner of the courtyard. There she watched, wide-eyed, as her father brought strange men into the house, from the servant's entrance. They gathered in the kitchen, where her father served them tea with trembling hands. There were seven men, including her father, and their voices batted back and forth, difficult to distinguish where one ended and the other began.

"His orders are insane," said one of the men. "He won't listen to any of us. If the Viziers can't succeed, what chance has the rest of Al-Rayyan?"

"He might listen to Munir," said another.

"Don't be absurd! That man is a coward, and everyone knows it. We need to show force. Force is what the Sultan respects."

"Your 'force' will see us all thrown into the dungeon, or worse," said another voice, quavering with age. "This wildness of his won't last. All things will pass away in time.
You'll see."

"But what of his command? To marry the women —?"

"Let him marry one from his harem," came Dunya's father's voice, solid and confident. "The most beautiful, or the most pleasing. For most men, that would calm them well enough. Let him try it."

"But what if he really orders her dead?"

There was a pause, and then Dunya's father said, "That is a risk we must take. After all, it's only one courtesan."

The finality of that phrase chilled Dunya, and, forgetting her hunger, she crept off to bed again.

The next morning, her father presided over the breakfast table, as lively and keen-eyed as if he had slept the sleep of the just. Dunya tried to tell herself that it had been a dream, but her knees were sore from where she had been crouching.

That night, he did not come home. His feet did not sound in the foyer until mid-morning. He called for tea, then for First Wife Noora. He spent hours in conference with her, and emerged looking none the better for it.

"This will pass. It must," said First Wife Noora.

"It must. It must," repeated Shareef.

Whatever it was, it did not pass. The days brought only greater stress and worry upon Shareef, and he paced so late into the night that Dunya doubted he got any kind of sleep. Finally, a kind of stoniness seemed to settle upon him: his eyes remained wide, his mouth set in an imperious frown, and he moved through life like a horse with blinders, limited in scope—and that scope was the Palace, and his home was merely where he slept.

A couple of months later, Dunya was up late, reading through the Sultana's prayer book again. She knew the prayers by heart now, but they were a little comfort. She had reached the end of the book when she heard her father stagger in.

Dunya very carefully tucked the book into her meager collection, and crept through the house until she found her father. He looked haggard and worn. Dunya was shy around him, but she could not let him sit there, so melancholy, without helping. She brought him a glass of sharbat and a plate of flaky pastries, and while he ate, she ventured to ask him what made him so afraid.

"I am only a daughter," she said, "and I know little, but perhaps I can help."

Her father spoke as if to himself, or to the empty air, as if he could not believe the words he was saying. "The Sultan has gone mad. His madness would destroy a lesser man; in him, it may destroy our Kingdom, too. He demands a gift from each of his Viziers, to show our heartfelt loyalty to him."

"Is there anything I could do?" Dunya asked.

As she said that, her father looked up at her. His eyes were ringed with dark circles, but a cunning look, the look of a politician, gleamed within them. "What would you do," he asked, "to help your father?"

"Anything," Dunya said. "I only want to help."

He stared somewhere past her, beyond her. "I must prove my loyalty to the Sultan," he said. "And you, with more filial piety than any other child of mine…you will help me."

"How?"

His eyes flitted to her and away. "Never you mind that. Go to bed. Tomorrow, wear your best. I will take you to the Palace."

Dunya's first thought was that she could return the book. It wasn't until she was safely in bed that she looked her fear in the eye. Her father had spoken of wildness—a wildness in the Sultan. And whatever had infected the Sultan might have infected the entire Palace.

"I must be brave," Dunya whispered, curled up close. "I must be brave."

In the morning, she dressed in the same blue dress and veil she had worn for the Sultan's wedding. She tucked the Sultana's prayer book into her belt and hated how her hands were shaking. She joined her father in the entrance hall, and they left her family's compound.

He led her through the gates, past the main building of the Palace with its screened windows, past the fountains and the glorious gardens. She was brought to a pavilion set apart from the main Palace, small and ivory-colored among the roses. Before the door there was an uneven stump of a small tree, the only ugly thing in sight. Dunya had a hard time tearing her eyes off of the stump—what was it doing there?—until her father dragged her into the pavilion.

Inside, the air was heavily perfumed, the sounds muffled by damask curtains and pillows. Screens were artfully arranged, blocking any way out.

Shareef's feet never strayed from their course. He found two women sitting opposite each other, a chessboard between them. He sat Dunya on the couch by them, forcibly.

"Now be good," he told her, "obey the guards, and listen to this woman here. Remember, you are doing your family, and your father, a great favor."

Dunya was so stunned she could not speak. She watched her father leave.

When the door shut, Dunya looked around. The two women stared at her. As her eyes adjusted to the dimness, she noticed lamps—mostly small, handheld lamps clustered in threes and fours on any available table. Not a single one was lit. Dunya drew her veil closer around her, and found herself hugging the Sultana's prayer book. She didn't belong here; she felt little and lost. She looked at the woman that her father had given her to. She had silver hair.

"I know you!" Dunya said with a gasp. "Morgiana!"

"Why, it's Munir's little find," said Morgiana. "I never thought I'd see you here."

"Please, ma'am, where am I?" Dunya asked.

The old woman laughed. "Such manners! Call me by my name. And you are in the Palace harem."

"The harem?" Dunya repeated. "Why would my father leave me in the harem?"

"Was that really your father?" asked the other woman, who knelt across the chessboard from Morgiana. "The Grand Vizier? I thought you were a girl he pulled in off the street." "Now, now," said Morgiana.

She fetched tea, and when she returned, Dunya said, "Last night, my father said that the Sultan had gone mad. Today he brought me here. Someone, please tell me what is going on."

So Morgiana explained. "The Sultana betrayed the Sultan. He found her in the arms of another man– her bodyguard. He slew her on the spot."

Dunya went cold, to the tips of her fingers. This was worse, much worse than the death she had imagined.

"I heard tell," said her opponent in chess, toying with a rook, "that the Vizier found the Sultan drenched in blood. I heard that the Sultan's only words to him were, 'It was over too quickly.'"

"Hush, Shirin," said Morgiana. "The Sultan has gone mad indeed. Having killed his first wife, he now picks his way through new brides. He takes one woman to be his Sultana each day; the concubine chosen is imprisoned in his bedchamber, until he visits her. At the next dawn, the Sultan leaves his chamber and orders his Sultana executed." "But why?" Dunya asked.

"Because he is the Sultan," answered Shirin.

"Because he wants to continue punishing his wife," Morgiana said.

"Because we are all the same to him," Shirin added.

"Because he is enamored of death," Morgiana finished. "The Sultan first married his female prisoners, and when he ran out of them he turned to the women of the harem.

There have been ninety-six women made into martyrs so far, including poor Yasmeen, taken just an hour hence. Before her it was Lironi, the prize of Jerusalem, and before that, Zumurrud of Samarkand. If the Sultan trusts his concubines so little, he must be demanding great shows of loyalty from his Viziers."

"You've just become a show of good faith, little girl," Shirin said, capturing a pawn.

In a small voice, Dunya said, "I am sorry for your plight."

"Do not be sorry for me," Morgiana replied. "I am not afraid. I am only sorry that your father used you in such a way."

"At this rate," Shirin observed, "you will be the ninetyninth of the Sultan's brides. How auspicious!"

Dunya started to cry. She would be sixteen in a month's time, and her own father had given her over to be a prisoner in the keep of a madman. Shirin stood up and walked to the window, and though Morgiana tried to comfort Dunya, she no longer told her to be brave.

Dunya barely slept that night. She woke up to the cricket-like sound of an ancient servant tottering into the harem before dawn. She lay where she was, curled still, and she heard Morgiana greet the serving-woman, who said, "Allah smiles upon you. The Sultan has announced that he will go hunting for lions and wild donkeys, on the advice of his Viziers. He will take no wife today."

"Not until he returns," said Shirin, sounding startlingly close to Dunya.

"What of Yasmeen?" Morgiana said. "Did the Sultan…" she trailed off.

"She died just a few moments ago," said the old woman. There was a pause, and she went on, "But you are spared! The hunt begins today and will last for two weeks, at least."

"And as long as the Sultan kills lions, his bloodlust is satisfied," Shirin spat.

"Shirin, you must curb your tongue," Morgiana said. "Perhaps the time in nature will soothe our Sultan's heart."

"There's more," said the old servant. "The other Viziers are putting out vast sums. I would guess they're trying to bring gifts, to buy themselves some security. You're not the only ones on the cutting block."

"In a very literal sense, we are," said Shirin, and Dunya felt inclined to agree with her.

"Grand Vizier Shareef has already given one of his most prized possessions. Can you guess, Nadirah?" This was Morgiana addressing the servant. "He has added his daughter to the harem."

"I'm not Father's prize possession," Dunya whispered into her hand. No one heard her.

"He's a smart man, then. But so are the other Viziers. Vizier Tariq has sent word to Munir, and asked him to bring back all the female prisoners from the border that he can muster."

"To give the Sultan more wives to slay?" Shirin asked. "That's not smart, that's cowardly!"

"Well, when you bite the King appointed by Heaven, I'll take you seriously, little viper," said Nadirah. "Now, what's my prize?"

There was a clink, clink, like chains or coins settling into place. "Allah bless and keep you," said Nadirah. "I will be back at nightfall."

Her footsteps faded away. There was a very loud rattle and clatter.

"Shirin!" Morgiana exclaimed. Dunya sat up to look. Shirin had taken the box that held a complete chess set, and spilled it out onto the floor. Then she picked up a second chess set, and spilled that out. She had just uncovered a third set under a pillow when Morgiana seized her.

"Stop that! You'll lose the pieces or break them. What are you doing?"

"What does it matter if they break?" Shirin replied. "My life has been nothing but misery ever since I entered this harem, and now I'm going to die without ever having known the slightest bit of liberty—"

"Wait a minute," said Dunya. Both of the women turned to look at her. "I thought my father was the only Vizier. Who are these others who are out writing letters and buying bribes?"

Shirin, still holding a chess game in one hand, started laughing. Morgiana joined in, and soon the two women were laughing so hard that they were crying and sitting down on the floor.

"It wasn't that funny," Dunya said, miffed.

"When I'm this afraid, everything is funny," said Shirin.

"You don't make any sense," said Dunya.

"And nor do you, little Miss Know-it-All," said Shirin. "Fancy a Vizier's daughter not knowing anything about politics!"

"Well, I don't!" Dunya could feel the tears starting up. "And I'm not my father's most prized possession. He only brought me here because I asked if I could help. What are you doing?"

"Giving you a lesson in politics." Shirin was on her knees now, picking up the discarded chess pieces and arranging them by type, rather than by color. "Listen up, Sultana-to-

Be. This—is the King." She held up the king piece. "The

Sultan."

"What do you remember of our chess lesson?" Morgiana asked Dunya.

"I remember enough," Dunya said. She planted herself on the other side of the game board. "Go on."

Shirin had gathered up a set of little war elephants. "These are the Viziers. Some of them inherited the position. Some married into it. Some actually earned it. They are also called Councilors, and they are supposed to advise the Sultan on various things…and they are supplemented," she gathered up the little cavaliers into a pile, "by the Guild leaders. There are guilds for merchants, guilds for alchemists, guilds for craftsmen…there's an entire guild dedicated purely to maintaining the river."

"What do they do?" Dunya asked, and then felt herself go pink. Shirin laughed again.

"Talking to you is an education! I'm glad you came along. We were very bored."

"Really?" Dunya asked. "I just find that hard to believe. Who are the Sultan's other advisors?"

Shirin paused. She paused long enough for Morgiana to say, "Maybe we should have a little breakfast before discussing this further—" and then Shirin unceremoniously shoved all of the pieces off of the carpet and set another king in the center of it and said, "and this is the only one that the Sultan listens to, and I mean the only one."

"Who is it?"

"It's the little voice inside of his head that says, 'Kill! Kill! Kill!'" Silence greeted this little pronouncement, but Shirin laughed at her own joke.

Morgiana sighed. "You're going to have to pick up all of those pieces, you know."

"No, no, I'll help," said Dunya.

"You don't have to—" Shirin started. "I'll help," Dunya said, her brow set.

Shirin let her help.

Dunya eventually gained the courage to ask, "What do you think Munir will do? When the other Vizier asks for prisoners of war?"

Shirin shrugged. "He'll probably oblige. He'd do anything to placate the Sultan."

"You don't know that," said Morgiana. "He may yet surprise us all."

"An unmarriageable cousin has a right to her opinion," said Shirin.

"You're Munir's cousin?" Dunya asked.

Shirin grinned wickedly. "I'm also Sultan Sayyid's cousin —I notice you didn't ask about him."

"Let her be," said Morgiana, while Dunya blushed. "We have been given a reprieve. We ought to be grateful for every minute of it."

"Oh, I am," said Shirin, putting the last pawn away in its box. "Is it too much to ask, though, to be hopeful as well? I had heard that Al-Rayyan was a city of magic, and where there is magic there is always hope. But no phoenix has burned the Sultan out, no shadhavar has gored him with its horn."

"Faith should be put in God alone," said Morgiana quietly. "We cannot see His entire plan, but that is no reason not to trust in Him."

"I would rather put my faith in…" Shirin rubbed her forehead and sighed. "An open road, a good pair of shoes, a pocketful of silver."

"Why don't you run away?" Dunya asked.

Morgiana and Shirin looked at one another again. "This harem is now more heavily guarded than any other part of the Palace, including the treasury," Morgiana said. "We have thought out a thousand and one ways, and they have come to nothing. We must have faith."

Shirin shook her head, her eyes furious.

Dunya looked at her hands, and thought, I will be sixteen and dead in a very short time. What will I make of what's left of my life?

Two weeks passed in a strange fashion—fear of what was to come made the time slip by, but the sheer boredom of life in the harem slowed time to a trickle. Shirin and Morgiana, though a strange pair, made good company. Dunya was mastering chess under their careful tutelage, when the Sultan returned.

Four of his bodyguards came to the harem. They frightened Dunya, these tall men with theirsharp eyes. Their gleaming swords separated Shirin as Dunya clung to Morgiana. An attendant covered Shirin with veils of red and white. They led her away. She was glimmering and beautiful, but with her jaw clamped shut, lest she curse the Sultan and his entire revered ancestry.

Dunya stared at the door after Shirin's departure. She started when Morgiana laid a hand on her shoulder.

"I'm sorry," Dunya stammered out.

"For what?" Morgiana asked.

Dunya drew the little prayer book out of her belt. "I've kept this hidden—I didn't want Shirin to see, because I thought she would laugh, but…it seems stupid now, doesn't it? Hiding it away… I'm sorry I hid it." She felt Morgiana's gaze and held the book up, as if in surrender. "It was a gift from the first Sultana," she said.

Morgiana gently took the book from Dunya's hands. "It's beautiful," she said. "Shirin would have loved it."

Dunya hugged herself close and tried to swallow her tears. "I should have shared it with her. But I was afraid she would…"

"Don't be so hard on yourself," Morgiana said. "Come, let's sit." When they were seated away from the door, Morgiana asked, "So this was a gift from the Sultan's first wife?"

"Yes." Dunya checked over her shoulder. "Father said not to mention her name…"

"Best not to, then."

"And it—wasn't a gift. It was a loan. But I never got to return it."

"Well, it's now in the Palace, where it belongs. Be at peace." Morgiana took the book from Dunya's hands and gently turned the pages until she arrived at a prayer asking for peace. "Do you want to pray?"

"Um, if you like," Dunya said. She was silent as Morgiana read the prayer and then clasped her hand in silence. Dunya looked in her heart, but didn't feel any special reverence or joy or peace—but she was glad to have Morgiana there.

Of course, Dunya realized, it couldn't last.

A few hours later, another pair of guards appeared at the door, and one of them—Dunya couldn't tell which—said, "Morgiana? Sultana Shirin asks for you."

"I may not be back," Morgiana said, getting to her feet.

"But it's not your time yet!" Dunya exclaimed.

"The Sultan," Morgiana said in a careful voice, "in his generosity, allows his wives to spend their time with a friend. I will send for you."

Dunya nodded, the words Please don't leave me stuck in her throat. She hugged Morgiana tight, but couldn't come up with anything elseto say. Morgiana left.

Dunya got very little sleep that night; rather, she fretted and paced. When the harem's braziers had burned down and the light of dawn filled the room, Dunya realized it was the day before her birthday.

"Shirin is dead," she repeated to herself, softly. "Morgiana will be dead tomorrow. And then… me."

She tried to pray, but peace and silence didn't come to her. It was a long and fruitless waiting period until the moment that the guards appeared at the door and asked for her, in the name of Sultana Morgiana.

Dunya hesitated, her hands on the prayer book. Should she bring it with her? Or…when one of the guards snapped at her to hurry up, she tucked the prayer book among the chess sets and hurried to join the guards.

Dunya followed the guards, barely aware of the route. When she crossed the final doorway, and saw Morgiana in a vast, splendid bedchamber, she cried out and ran to her.

"As Sultana, I welcome you, for what it is worth," said

Morgiana. "I understand it is your birthday?"

Dunya said that it was. Morgiana ordered the Palace servants to bring out pastries and wine, as haughtily as if she had been doing this all her life. She relaxed onto the cushions of silk from distant China, and gestured through the cedar screen to the Palace gardens.

"Look at this splendor. Such glory and grandeur! But I miss Shirin. Oh, you don't believe me?" She smiled at the look on Dunya's face. "She was a friend. Without her, this landscape suffers." Morgiana sighed. "I've walked every inch of these grounds. I have found many marvels. In the garden, there is a fountain that spurts water so cold it burns. In the Palace's basement, there is a carpet, woven in red and black. It has a great magic in it…though I've never been able to name what that magic is. There is…well, there

was the tree whose leaves sang lullabies."

"I remember that tree."

"It was cut down…I'm sure you can imagine. But even with that loss, what a place to live in! A scholar would dream of finding such a menagerie of wonders. But I have never wanted anything more than freedom."

"I understand…" Dunya murmured. She settled herself uneasily onto the couch. Looking around, she felt a jolt of shock.

"What is it?" Morgiana asked.

"That mirror…" Dunya pointed, "The one hanging opposite the bed. My father bought that mirror for the Sultan's marriage. I was there when he bought it." On a whim, she added, "The seller was not a human, though. It was a nasnas—only a right half of a human being, and the inside all like rough gems. You know," she grabbed a lock of her hair and played with it, "I've never told anyone else that before. No one else saw that the mirror seller was not human."

"I'm honored that you told me," said Morgiana.

"Well, of course. You believe in magic. I thought you only believed in God?"

Morgiana shrugged. "All kinds of forces are at play in this world. I have a passing acquaintance with many of them…not that it ever did me any good. There was a time— oh, when I was a little girl—I thought that the sea was the greatest power in the world. But I haven't seen it in so many years. Have you ever seen the sea? I sometimes worry that even I have forgotten what it was really like."

"How did you come to be here?" asked Dunya.

"I was captured as a prisoner of war. I was brought here to grace the bed of the previous Sultan, but instead, he left me to languish and wait. Like thieves, forty years have taken away bits of my life. But I am not afraid. Come tomorrow, I will be at last free. I hope you will have a pleasant Feast of Sacrifices, and a wonderful birthday."

After that, the Sultan arrived. He entered the bedchamber, tall and forbidding, and sent Dunya away without even looking at her. Two of the Sultan's bodyguards escorted her back to the empty harem.

She did not sleep that night.

At sunrise, the old servant, Nadirah, arrived to tell Dunya that Morgiana had died. Dunya, who'd thought she was all wrung out, cried some more at this news. All the while, Nadirah stood there, faintly embarrassed, waiting for her tip. Dunya had nothing except her gold earrings, so she gave away those. She wouldn't need them anymore.

At noon, the soldiers and attendants came to the harem. The attendants wrapped Dunya in red and white veils. Trembling like a rose in a storm, she was brought before the Sultan, and a holy man. Some prayers and promises were said, and just like that, she was Dunya, the little Sultana.

With the title of Sultana came immediate responsibilities. To fulfill her spiritual obligations, she was guided to the royal mosque under armed guard, to honor the Feast of the Sacrifice.

She felt ridiculous in her new veils, leading the procession as if she fit in there. But she could be silent, and when the imam began to lead prayer, she gave a sigh of relief. Listening, that was a skill she had long since mastered. She listened to his words, and prayed as well as she could, while trying to order her tormented soul to be peaceful.

The imam, in his prayer, recounted the day when Abraham bound his beloved son Ismail to the altar rock to be sacrificed before Allah. At the last moment, Allah sent an angel to stay Abraham's knife. But Dunya's mind lingered on the image of the ram with its horns tangled in thorns. Did the ram think that was fair? Was the ram grateful to Allah?

Silently, Dunya the Sultana prayed for the souls of Morgiana, Shirin, and the others; she prayed for her family; but in her most honest heart, she prayed that Allah would send a way to save her.

Night fell. Dunya had to preside over a feast where she could not eat a morsel. Her father was there, and he did not acknowledge her in any way. Dunya did not even bother trying to get his attention—aside, of course, from sitting at his side swamped in rich fabrics.

The Sultana did not look at her husband, and she did not look at her father, either. She spent most of her time watching the door, hoping against hope that something extraordinary would happen. But, a phoenix did not appear, nor did a furious shadhavar–not even so much as a nasnas. And all Dunya could think about was, I will die in the morning.

When the feast was over, the Sultana had to retire to her rooms. Dunya entered the bedchamber, just as luxurious and beautiful and perfect as it had been the night before, with the same mirror twinkling on the wall opposite the bed.

Servants arrived, removed her finery, and helped her to dress for bed in what she assumed were a dead woman's clothes. She shivered when the servants left, and took herself to the window seat—just where Morgiana had sat.

It had been a long day, and she was very tired. She laid her head down on the pillow and fell asleep as the stars came out.

She woke up suddenly. The lanterns were dim, the starlight was bright in the room, and there was a strange woman in the bedchamber with her.

"Do not be afraid," the woman said, before Dunya could cry out. "I am here to help you."

And Dunya, looking at the woman, was not afraid. The woman was very beautiful. She was tall and strong beneath rich black robes glinting with silver. Her hair was black and glossy, and her eyes were as brilliant as diamonds.

"Who are you?" Dunya asked.

"I have been watching over you since the day you were born, young Dunya," said the woman, with a gentle smile.

"What is your name?" Dunya was now quite confused.

"You may call me Zahra," the woman answered. "May I presume to make a request?"

Dunya, bewildered and wondering if the woman could have possibly scaled the Palace walls, nodded.

"When the Sultan has arrived and is at ease, ask that I tell you a story. Do you like stories?" Zahra asked.

Before Dunya could answer (or ask another question), the Sultan entered. His eyes were full of anger, despite the sanctity of the night. He shed his robes of state like a snake shedding his skin. As he passed into the bedchamber, he looked around for his bride.

Dunya shrank back, afraid of him, but Zahra stepped forward, greeted him, and said, "Husband." Sultan Sayyid looked at her.

"You're Shareef's daughter? From this morning? You seemed shorter then." He pointed to Dunya, curled up against the screen. "You. I've met you..."

"You remember her, but not me?" Zahra asked. "She is my little sister, come to keep me company in my last hours. We are the both the daughters of your faithful Vizier. My modesty obliged me to remain in our Father's house and care for him." She was so graceful, so elegant, that the man forgot the small lady in the corner entirely.

After a time, when Zahra's charms failed to move him any longer, the Sultan took himself to a table, set against the western wall. He pulled a cloth away to uncover a tray full of silver blades, all shapes and sizes, glinting in the lamplight. He picked the instruments up, one by one, and toyed with them.

Dunya started to breathe too quickly, fear stealing her breath; she was regarding the Sultan, the man sitting not even ten feet away from her, with a low hum of horror. It was horribly easy to imagine the Sultan killing his first wife. He had sent ninety-eight women to their deaths, killing them as surely as if the executioner's blade was in his hand. Dunya couldn't help but remember what Shirin had said— that the only statement the Sultan made after killing his wife was, "It was over too quickly."

And yet Zahra did not seem perturbed at all. She called for wine to be poured, and asked Dunya to sit at her knee. As Dunya settled herself comfortably, she looked up at

Zahra—uncertain if she was looking at a blessing from God, or a cunning thief, or maybe both—and asked, "Sister, would you please tell me a story?"

"If the Sultan does not object," Zahra answered.

The Sultan did not object, but waved his hand in a generous gesture. He turned to them, now sharpening a blade with a whetstone.

"Dunya," Zahra looked at the girl with a sly and curious expression, "do you know the story of Ali Baba, the forty thieves, and the slave girl?"

Dunya shook her head. And Zahra began her story.

There was once a poor woodcutter named Ali Baba, who chanced upon a bandit's treasure trove. Ali Baba stole their gold with the help of the magic words, "Open, Sesame!"

But what had at first seemed like a marvelous boon turned into a deadly threat. Ali Baba told his brother, Caseem, about the treasure, and against Ali Baba's warning, Caseem sought out the cave himself. In his delight at finding more gold than he could fit into his saddlebags, Caseem forgot the magic words to leave the cave.

Well, Caseem reasoned, in his gold-filled prison, he could fight off the cave's owner. He was a strong man, he could take a cowardly bandit or two. But when he heard the words "Open, Sesame!" the door opened to reveal forty thieves. They stared in surprise at an intruder in their treasury—but they weren't surprised for long.

After three days, Ali Baba sought out Caseem at the cave, and he found his elder brother murdered—in a manner most gruesome—for his greed. Ali Baba retrieved his brother's body, took him home for burial, and put out word that Caseem had died of a sudden illness. Now, all that had been the brother's belonged to Ali Baba—and first among these assets was a slave girl, known to be both brave and clever, whose name was Morgiana.

Dunya lost her breath, but the Sultan did not react in any visible way. And Zahra continued her tale....

Ali Baba grieved for his brother, but he could not forget that the bandits would want to track down whoever had taken Caseem's body away. His grief was terrible, but he noticed that the dead man's slave had dry eyes and a clear head. So Ali Baba took Morgiana into his counsel, explained their dire situation in full, and trusted her to choose the best course of action to outwit the bandit leader and his thirtynine thieves. Morgiana shirked from no task, no matter how gruesome, but the thieves were also fairly clever.

The leader of the theives, eager to reclaim his stolen loot, asked for a volunteer to trace the man who had found his way into their stronghold. The bravest of the thieves eagerly accepted the task. The young man traced the gold to Ali Baba's house, and under the noonday sun marked Ali Baba's door with chalk, so that the thieves could find it again at night. Then as the sun set, Morgiana marked every door in the district with chalk. The bravest of the thieves was executed for his stupidity.

That thief's brother, eager to restore the family honor, volunteered next to find Ali Baba's house, and the stolen gold. He successfully retraced his brother's route, and chipped away a piece of the stone stair leading to Ali Baba's door. But Morgiana saw him, and she had tools of her own. She wasted no time, chipping away at the stones of every house in the neighborhood, and a few others besides. The thief tasked with finding the door was also executed, joining his brother in eternal frustration.

But on the third try, the bandit leader took the task on himself. He found Ali Baba's house, and he memorized every part of the door and its location so he would not forget it. And on that very night...

At that very moment, the rising sun entered the chamber. Zahra fell silent.

Dunya had leaned close to the storyteller, hanging on to every word, and, now that the words had ceased, hanging on to silence. Even the Sultan was sitting on the side of the bed, his eyes wide and staring.

"Well?" the Sultan asked. "Go on! What happened next?"

"My Lord, I do not have time," Zahra replied, dropping her eyes. The bold elocutionist had vanished, replaced by a meek, obedient, perfect wife. "The sun has risen. It is time for my execution."

And so it was. Already the Sultan's guards were assembling to escort the Sultana to her doom.

The Sultan strode to Zahra and, seizing her by the shoulders, shook her. "You will finish the story! I am the

Sultan! I command it!"

"But my Lord, the story will take hours. You have many duties that await you. Even now, I hear the call to prayer." Zahra's voice was reverent and low. "You will likely need breakfast and a short rest. My Lord, I assure you, I would rather die than cause you the slightest inconvenience."

They stood there, at a stalemate, until Dunya had an idea. She said, "My Lord? You could spare her—my sister, that is—for today. And she can finish the story tonight."

She dearly wanted to know what became of Morgiana and the forty (now thirty-eight) thieves.

The Sultan paused, then leapt upon the idea. "Spare her? Yes. Yes! I will spare her. Guards!"

The guards and the Grand Vizier entered the chamber. Dunya drew back at the sight of her father.

The Sultan pointed to Zahra. He commanded, "Keep a watch on this wife of mine. See to it that no man enters and that she does not leave this chamber."

"But what about the sentence of execution?" the Vizier asked, cautiously.

"For today, it is suspended. But only for today."

The Sultan left at once, and Dunya felt relief sweep through her. She clapped her hands to her mouth and might have laughed out loud were it not for the presence of her father. He was looking at Zahra, and his next words stunned Dunya speechless:

"You are a lucky, lucky woman, Your Highness." "Highness?" Dunya repeated.

Shareef looked at her. "Dunya? What are you doing here? Why aren't you in the harem?"

"Don't you remember, Papa?" asked Zahra. "I asked Dunya to come with me and listen to my stories. If she were not here, I might not be alive."

Now Dunya fell silent, while she watched her father chuckle and shake his head at Zahra, as he'd done at his eldest daughter's wedding. "If you say so. Pray to the

Almighty that your luck continues." "I am not

afraid," she said.

Vizier Shareef looked between the two of them, and then the Sultan yelled for him from down the hall. The Vizier left quickly, and Dunya got to her feet. Her head was spinning.

"You," she said to Zahra. "You are not the Sultana. I am. I am sure of that."

"Good. Certainty is a virtue in a young lady."

"And you—you might be my father's daughter," she allowed, "But you are certainly no sister that I know. Why did you say that you were? Why did my father know you?"

"I am known to all," said Zahra. "And memories are an easy thing to confuse."

"I don't understand."

"You do not need to. Not yet. But rest assured: as long as you are my sister, you will live."

At those words, Dunya was afraid again. She could almost see the executioner's blade glinting in the light. "I want to live," she said, "I'll call you my sister, if that's what you want. But I'll remember..." she trailed off.

"Good. Remember the truth. And now, I suggest that you sleep."

Dunya tottered, suddenly exhausted. "Yes. Sleep."

There was a little chamber adjoining the grand Sultan's bedchamber. Zahra guided Dunya into this room, while Dunya asked, "Has this always been here?" Soon Dunya was lying on the bed, her thoughts unraveling. She felt a deep happiness at being alive, being sleepy—hearing the songbirds, lying in the sunlight, feeling the breeze and the sounds of the Palace coming awake. Then she slept.

The Storyteller

Dunya woke up in the afternoon, wondering where she was. Then she remembered Morgiana, and her heart ached, but Zahra was in the bedroom with her, standing by the window. So Dunya forced herself awake, to face the day. She ventured past the door of the bedroom, past the tall guards. She stepped slowly and fearfully, but they did not stop her. She found her way to the kitchens and politely asked the chef for food.

The chef, charmed by her manners, let her take whatever she liked. She piled a plate high with her favorites —nuts and dates, spiced lamb pies, and pickled beets. She had had a very trying few days, she told herself, and deserved something nice.

She took her food back to the bedchamber and offered some to Zahra.

Zahra was reading a scroll and did not appear to have rested at all, but she was still as beautiful as ever. She took two dates and two almonds, but refused any more, thanking Dunya for her kindness.

Dunya, however, was not satisfied by this good act. She observed Zahra closely for sometime. Then she went to the window and looked down. A sheer drop of white stone greeted her. It would be impossible to climb up.

Dunya sniffed and fidgeted, pondered Zahra, and contemplated her own change in fortune. She was happy to be alive another day, no question about that, but there was something almost too lucky about Zahra's arrival. One reversal of fortune—married to the Sultan!—was paired with another—the Sultan was insane! And who was to say that this one—mysterious stranger at the last possible moment— wouldn't be paired with a price that was even worse?

Best, then, to be prepared. Dunya decided to go on the offense, springing questions on Zahra like a hunter with his traps—all equally ineffectual.

"When did you sleep?" she asked Zahra.

"When you slept," Zahra replied.

"How did you enter the Palace?"

"By the front door."

"Did you bring any robes other than those black ones?"

"I did not."

"How long will you stay here, then?"

"For as long as I am needed."

"With only one change of clothes? Why those robes, then?"

"They're comfortable and I like them."

"But why are they embroidered all over with little silvery eyes?"

Zahra regarded the fabric. "I think they're pretty." And, well, Dunya could hardly argue with that.

"Have you left this room at all today?"

"No."

"Why not?"

"Because the Sultan commanded that his wife stay here."

"You are not the Sultan's wife," Dunya said. "I am."

"Is that so?"

"I don't want to be, but I remember. Where did you come from?"

"God created me."

"Why did you come here?"

"I thought it was a good idea."

"That's not an answer! If you don't give me any answers, I'll have to make up my own."

"I don't mind."

Dunya leaned on the bed and stared hard at Zahra, her imagination working as hard as she could make it. "You are from a noble family which has lost all of its money in recent generations. You grew up poor, but proud, and very clever. With no suitors on your hand, you turned to mischief. When you heard of Sultan Sayyid's madness, you thought, 'Aha! Here's a challenge worthy of my steel.' So you prepared your stories, climbed the castle walls…snuck in past the guards…I don't know."

"That was enjoyable. Tell me another one when you invent it."

"Tonight, the Sultan will return. Will you continue Morgiana's story?"

"Yes."

"And how will you survive when that is done?"

"I have a plan."

Dunya frowned. By now she was restless, so she bid Zahra good afternoon and went to wander the palace. She avoided clumps of people, and passed long hours in a fine, open garden brimming with ponds and lotuses. After evening prayers, she found her way to the Palace's dining hall, where the Sultan, the courtiers, and the Viziers took their supper. There was plenty of food for her, and when dinner was finished, she followed the Sultan up to his chambers.

There they found Zahra, sitting by the window. The Sultan threw himself on the bed and commanded Zahra, "Now, you will finish the story!"

"Of course," Zahra said, smiling again. "But first— Dunya, come sit by my knee."

Dunya knelt by Zahra, and she felt a peculiar rapture when Zahra looked down at her and picked up the tale.

Morgiana outwitted the bandit leader yet again: The leader prepared an ambush, setting thirty-eight vast oil jugs in Ali Baba's house, each jug holding a bloodthirsty thief. But Morgiana heated a vast amount of olive oil until it was boiling and, with no mercy or hesitation, filled the jugs, one by one, with the oil. The bandit leader caught the stench of burning flesh and fled in terror.

To honor Morgiana's guile and courage, Ali Baba set her free—but Morgiana still worked in the household of Ali Baba, for after all, how could a slave possibly be expected to navigate the wide world, with the sudden gift of freedom?

"Quite so, quite so," the Sultan said, nodding at the comment. "Slaves and dogs are kept close, for their own protection." But the story wasn't yet finished.

With a rich costume for disguise and a dagger at his waist, the bandit leader returned to Ali Baba's house, craving revenge. Ali Baba, giddy over his new wealth, welcomed the man, but Morgiana recognized the bandit leader at once.

For a disguise, she dressed as a dancer, with a dagger of her own tucked away. After dinner, she presented herself as the evening's entertainment. With a simpering smile, she spun and twirled closer to Ali Baba and his guest of honor, while the music rose and the flames flickered, until, with a gleam and a cry, her dagger found its place in the bandit leader's heart. Morgiana ceased her dance and, with a bow to Ali Baba, drew off the villain's disguise.

In awe and in gratitude, Ali Baba embraced Morgiana as his daughter, and gave her a filial share of his fortune. And they all lived quite happily ever after.

The Sultan thought that to be a needlessly sentimental ending, but Dunya was almost ready to cry. She was so happy to hear that Morgiana—even a Morgiana within a tale —had won her freedom and a high place in the world. With this, Dunya's heart eased, a little, from its grief.

"Would you like to hear another tale?" Zahra asked.

"Yes!" said Dunya and the Sultan at once.

And so Zahra began another story...

There was once a girl of the steppe, whose dowry was her sharp tongue and three bundles of fleece. This daughter's name was Shirin, and she wanted a wider future for herself.

Shirin lived with a large family in the middle of the lonely steppe. One year, on the coldest day in winter, a great Falcon the size of a horse landed before the herdsman's hut. The Falcon demanded to speak to the herdsman. The Falcon told the herdsman that he would grow rich and prosperous if he would give her his youngest daughter to be the Falcon's own friend.

The herdsman, not being a sentimental sort, agreed to this. Shirin was sad to say goodbye to her family, but when she looked up at the Falcon she could see her future opening up, and it was with a willing heart that she climbed aboard the Falcon's back and held on as they flew away.

The Falcon took Shirin to a magnificent house high in the mountains, where the wind piped music all day and the walls were always warm. The Falcon instructed Shirin that she was to be granted all the freedom of the lady of the house, but when night fell, Shirin must obey strict rules—the first and last of which was that she must not look at the Falcon herself, after nightfall. Shirin, pleased with her new estate, agreed to these rules at once.

The days passed pleasantly. Shirin relished the freedom of her new home and, in the evenings, sitting behind a screen in a semi-lit room, the Falcon would join her for readings of poetry and sips of wine. In the morning, the Falcon was always gone.

For a time, Shirin was happy with her new life. But she began to grow bored with the solitude, and she missed the presence of her many siblings and the family she had left behind. And although the Falcon grew dear to her, Shirin turned vexed that she could not see the Falcon at night— when she was sure that her hostess changed shape.

After a year and a day, the Falcon took pity on Shirin's loneliness and promised to take her back to her family for a visit, but warned her, "Only listen to them with half a heart."

But Shirin was feeling contrary, and when her sisters warned her that the Falcon was planning on eating her up, and her brothers warned her that she was living with a monster, she listened with all her heart. Her sisters gave her a lamp, her brothers gave her flint, and her mother gave her a knife. Concealing all three, she returned to her home with the Falcon in the mountains.

In the palace of the Sultan, the sun rose.

Zahra fell silent once again. The Sultan's guards were late in arriving, as if anticipating that they would not be needed. The Sultan told them that he would send for them when he required their services.

"You are a good tale-spinner, wife," he said to Zahra. "And you..." he growled at Dunya. "Leave me in peace. I need to get some sleep before I get to work."

Dunya left him, and she slept herself. When she awoke, she went down to the Palace dining hall for lunch, and then retreated to the great Library, to exult in its thousands of books and even read one or two. But she was quick to return to the Sultan's bedchamber at sunset. Zahra was sitting before the mirror, combing out her hair. She had washed and dressed in a deep blue gown, one that suited the station of a Sultana.

"You seem very comfortable in this role," said Dunya, crossing the room to sit on the bed.

"What role do you mean?" Zahra asked her.

"The Sultana. Some girls are raised all their lives to become Sultana. Were you one of them?"

"Not precisely."

"Then who are you?"

"I was raised to be a servant," Zahra said, "if you can believe that."

Dunya narrowed her eyes at Zahra, trying to imagine her in the livery of a household servant. "That's hard to believe. I have another question. Where do you get your stories from?"

Zahra merely glanced at her.

Dunya went on, "Do you know that the women in your stories—those are the names of women from the harem. Women who died. Do you know that? Why are those the names of women in your stories? Where do your stories come from?"

Zahra was silent for a moment, then she said, "I believe in honoring the dead. As for my stories, they are reflections of the world that we know. Most stories are. These stories reflect the world as it might have been, had things been different."

"You mean you make them up."

"If you say so."

"That's not to say that I don't like them," Dunya offered, after a pause. "I do. I like them very much. I really like not dying," she added, "but your stories make me think of the women I knew. And that makes me happy."

"I really make you happy?" Zahra asked, turning to look at Dunya. She was smiling, and it was a peculiarly earnest and winsome smile.

"Your stories make me very happy. I just hope that Shirin doesn't play the fool and end up in a bad way." "You'll see," was Zahra's response.

The Sultan came into the room at that point, and Dunya went silent. She posed herself at Zahra's knee, and said, as if by rote, "Sister, will you please continue last night's story?"

"Of course, little Dunya," was Zahra's reply. "So..."

There came the night when Shirin decided to end the Falcon's charade once and for all. She struck the flint and lit the lamp, and when she held the dagger aloft, she found not a monster, but a beautiful woman in the Falcon's place—a woman with fierce golden eyes and a fluting voice that Shirin loved.

The Falcon was furious at Shirin's disobeying. She scolded Shirin as though she were a child, and Shirin lashed back, citing how unfair and trying the Falcon's treatment had been. "How did you expect me to trust you, if you lied to me about your true nature?"

To which the Falcon replied, "I was relying on your trust, not your scorn. I shall have to fly away now, to the land beyond the North Star, and I shall never see you again."

At once Shirin regretted her rash words and begged the Falcon to stay, But the Falcon took to the air and flew off, and as soon as she was gone, the beautiful home on the mountain vanished, leaving Shirin cold, shivering, and far from any home.

Shirin did not point her shoes towards the herdsman's hut. Instead, she resolved to go to the land beyond the North Star and seek out the shape-shifter that she knew and loved.

The way was long and treacherous. Shirin sought the help of the Four Winds, but they all said that she was no sort of lady for them to help, being neither modest, nor quiet, nor pious. Finally, she sought out the most wicked, most powerful djinn she could find. Finally, after she spoke to six sinful djinn, they led her to their sister, the Djinni of Pride, who was strong enough to take Shirin beyond the North Star, and who, furthermore, would never turn down a challenge.

Far beyond the North Star, Shirin and the Djinni of Pride found a palace made of the northern lights and the coldest, purest ice. There lived a tribe of ferocious efreets, all abuzz with preparations for a great wedding. Their prince was to be married to a princess who had been cursed years ago into the shape of a Falcon, unless she should either agree to marry the Prince or find a human girl willing to marry her.

And so Shirin learned the story of her dear Falconwoman, and she grew even more determined than before: she would rescue her Falcon and somehow return to the land that they knew.

At this point in the story, the sun rose and again Zahra stopped talking. Again, the Sultan pardoned her, and went to nap in an evil mood. Dunya napped herself, and passed another pleasant day in the library. Around dinnertime, Dunya passed through one of the Palace gardens, and there, she was surprised to meet Zahra, accompanied by half of the Sultan's elite guard. Dunya fell into step alongside her "sister," and spoke to her in an undertone.

"You have a plan. I'm starting to see it, now."

"Is that so?"

"Every night, a long, wonderful story. Every dawn, an intolerable ending. Every night, the story picks up, but then another one starts. You've stayed alive longer than anyone else has."

"We have both stayed alive."

"Oh, I am grateful to you, very grateful…I just wonder, how long do you think you can keep doing it?"

Zahra smiled at Dunya, with a cunning, secretive grin. "I have a lot of stories."

"This is hardly what anyone would call a marriage."

"Let us return. The sun is going down," Zahra said. As they turned, she added, "A marriage is a shared, made-up thing. Most of life is made up as one goes along, dear."

"Are your stories made up as you go along?" said Dunya.

"They come to me, rather," said Zahra.

"You don't make any sense."

"But I keep us alive," said Zahra. "Now, come. This story has a very good conclusion."

They returned to the Sultan's suite. This time, he was waiting for them, and he tapped his foot impatiently while Zahra slowly prepared herself and finally settled down among the pillows. Dunya prompted Zahra, and she continued the story.

Shirin was determined to stop the wedding. With cunning, bribery, and a small use of brute force, she smuggled her way into the Falcon-princess's bedroom late at night. Her Falcon recognized her immediately, but they were shy around one other, each remembering the angry words they had shouted in their last meeting. Finally, Shirin tried to apologize at the same time as the Falcon-princess. At the end, they clasped hands and forgave one another.

Then, they hatched a plan together.

On the day of the wedding, the Falcon-princess declared that she wanted to set a final, simple challenge for her fiancé to complete. She challenged the efreet-prince to successfully shepherd a herd of caribou into a pack on the palace grounds. The efreet did his best, but his height and voice—and the flames that erupted constantly from his back —terrified the poor beasts, and he stormed off in a furious temper, saying no one could have done better.

"I bet that she could do better," said the Falconprincess, pointing to Shirin, who was sitting by the palace gate.

Shirin, confident in herself, got to her feet and roamed the tundra, bringing the caribou to their pens with love and patience. The efreet-prince and his whole court were so furious that they tore themselves to pieces, and Shirin could finally embrace her Falcon-princess. The Djinni of Pride took them back to the land that they knew..

There, Zahra assured the Sultan and Dunya, they lived in mutual love and respect for many years.

"Humph," said the Sultan. "I didn't trust that story from the moment the Falcon opened its mouth. I have so little patience with magic in a story."

"Then perhaps you shall enjoy another tale," Zahra offered, "one with no magic whatsoever—simply a story of a courtesan named Yasmeen. What do you say?"

The Sultan eagerly agreed and asked to hear the story.

Dunya's days fell into a pattern: long nights of listening to Zahra speak, and then sleep in the early hours of the morning, waking up when the sun was high. The hours in between, she wandered the library or the gardens, or strayed close to the groups of courtiers, listening to their talk. When they were not composing poems or commissioning paintings, they were discussing the beauty and mystery of the new Sultana, she who was rarely seen. No one seemed to realize that Zahra was an imposter. It was a strange magic.

Dunya remembered the sight of the nasnas, and the fact that all it took was a display of pretty mirrors to keep her family from looking, really looking, at the half-person right before their eyes. Perhaps there was no magic at the heart of this, merely exhaustion from an indifferent court... but, then again, perhaps there was.

Pah. Dunya had heard enough and thought of this enough. She did not wish to be a Sultana—not when Morgiana and Shirin's blood stained the title. The sister of the current Sultana, now that was suitable. A Princess. A Princess without guards, without retinue, without attendants. A Princess able to choose how she would spend her days.

The library was a wonder, and the gardens were a delight, but more and more she strayed to the walls of the Palace, to look over at the river flowing north to south, and at the city that rose on all sides. In her daily routine, she grew accustomed to the strangeness of Zahra, who now appeared quite at home in the Palace. The woman had ordered the Palace to her own liking: from the dressmakers, she ordered new clothes, from the treasury, she requested an allowance, and from the library, she requested books. The allowance she gave to Dunya; the books and the fabrics occupied her own days.

But busy as Zahra was, in her own subdued way, it seemed that little escaped her notice.

One evening, as Dunya and Zahra were waiting for the arrival of the Sultan, Dunya stared out the window at the lights of Al-Rayyan. "You know, life is really quite short" Zahra said,

"I do know that," said Dunya. "I've had a lot of time to think about my own death, you know, before you arrived."

Zahra did not take offense—she never took offense. Instead, she smiled and said, "All I mean is that if you long to see the city, you should go and explore, while the time is yours."

At the very suggestion of what she had wanted, Dunya balked. She turned to Zahra and said, "I don't know. It would be so easy to get lost, and there are many dangers for a young girl...at least, that's what my father always said."

"You are not quite a young girl, though. You are old enough to cover your hair, for instance."

"I suppose..." Dunya found herself gnawing on a fingernail. Her hair had never been important up until now, either in the walls of her father's house or sequestered in the harem.

"Wait here." Zahra went to her dresser and brought back a headscarf. It was not black, but blue, with faint stripes. Strange that it had been made for a Sultana, but was simple enough to belong to almost any girl of AlRayyan. "Try this," she said. She helped Dunya fit it over her long hair and tuck it behind her ears. The fabric was soft and light. Dunya went to the mirror to look at herself. With the veil over her hair, she felt suddenly more grown-up.

"That's better," said Zahra. "Go quietly and carefully, and you will not be seen unless you want to be seen."

Dunya peered at her sidelong. "The way you are talking, saying...Is that magic?"

"If you think it is so, then it is so," came Zahra's reply. "I think the blue looks good on you."

And maybe it was magic, or maybe it was just Dunya's nature as a quiet girl, but from then on, when she wore Zahra's headscarf, she seemed nearly invisible. From guards to servants to Viziers, nobody seemed to notice her. With it, she wandered the rooms of the Palace and, one day, climbed to the top of the Palace walls. She looked out over Al-Rayyan, wishing to go into the city.

Again and again, she found herself ascending the wall and looking out over Al-Rayyan. The city was made of red stone, with rare canals sparkling between the streets. The brilliant domes and tiles of the rooftops were humbled by lines of washing that crisscrossed the air. The people who crowded the streets and bridges were so distant, Dunya couldn't make them out, but she yearned to join them.

She rested her elbows on the wall and muttered, "But how to get out? I must be able to return every night. I don't want to miss Zahra's wonderful stories."

A company of horsemen parading down an avenue gave her an idea. She could follow the couriers out, perhaps even take a horse of her own! She took up her skirts and descended the wall, going in search of the stables.

She found them eventually, when the sun was setting. And Dunya learned something new, just being there: horses scared her. Their size dwarfed her, and they seemed wild, their shining hooves all to eager to kick out. Dunya was looking for a way back to the palace proper when another rider arrived – this one was a courier.

The courier addressed the palace steward, saying "I bring letters from Munir. One for the Sultan, and one for the Grand Vizier."

Dunya's interest was caught. Still, no one seemed to notice her, so she followed the track of the second letter as the steward took it to the Grand Vizier's office. Shareef was there, surrounded by papers and talking to another Vizier. Shareef took the letter.

Dunya paused outside the door. Some barriers she didn't want to test. She slipped out of sight, and heard her father opening the scroll, and then a thwack. He must have laid it aside.

"Any news?" asked the other Vizier. Dunya didn't know him. It was infuriating, how much she didn't know.

"He's a damned hypocrite. Says we're weak-livered for letting the Sultan's madness get to this point—but he says so on paper, a safe week's ride away from the Palace."

"What else is new?" asked the other Vizier. "Does he plan on visiting soon?"

"He asks us to keep him informed. He must not have received my latest letter, then. No plans on visiting. As ever, we're on our own. Coward."

Dunya didn't want to hear this. She started to creep away, and then heard her father yell, "Dunya!"

Damnation. So someone had noticed her, after all.

She turned around and said, "Yes, Father?"

"The Sultan seems less inclined to kill you these days," he said casually, "Do you think you could bring up a delicate subject to him?"

"What?" Dunya was confused.

"The Sultan is growing more distracted," he explained. "He is paying less and less notice to the affairs of his Kingdom. If you could persuade him, as his sister-in-law, to talk to us, his council of Viziers, that would do a great deal of good..."

"He barely notices me," Dunya told them. "And I am his wife."

But her father waved a hand, already turning away. "I knew I could trust you to do it. Go on, then."

Dunya left and followed the track of the second letter, sent to the Sultan's chambers. Dunya trembled as she approached the doors, hoping that Zahra would be there.

Mysterious Zahra, who had saved her life.

She entered and found Zahra lounging with the Sultan on the bed. There was an energy in the air that Dunya didn't recognize and didn't like. But there was also a sumptuous dinner set out on a side table, and Zahra told Dunya to help herself. The Sultan didn't notice her—he was reading from a scroll.

"Listen to this!" the Sultan said. "Munir says that he agrees with me that all women are faithless and heartless…"

"Present company excluded?" Zahra asked, leaning over to stroke his hand. Dunya shuddered.

"Oh, you're a fool indeed if you think I trust you," the Sultan said with a laugh. Zahra's playful smile died on her lips. "Oh, now Munir starts to flatter me. He was always weak. But he hasn't got any bright ideas about usurping me, at least he's that smart…" He noticed Dunya for the first time. "You! What are you doing here?"

Dunya had been lost in memories of Munir, from the one time she had met him, but she cleared her head enough to say "I'm here to listen to a story from my…sister. How does the story of Yasmeen end?"

"You may find out tonight," Zahra said, teasing out a lock of her black hair. "And then again, you might not."

The Sultan grunted, and Dunya remembered her father's words. "By the way, my Lord, the Grand Vizier Shareef has...erm...he's asked if you might...consider... possibly..." Her fear overwhelmed her and the rest of the words spilled out, "...paying more attention to the city's affairs?"

He turned to her, and his eyes were terrible. "Why, you presumptuous little —"he began to berate her, with such fury and language that Dunya was sure he would command her death. He finished by reaching over and smacking her head, saying, "If you are so intent on the affairs of the Kingdom,

you can run them, you ignorant worm!"

He turned his back to her. "Go on!" he barked at Zahra. "Tell us what happened to Yasmeen."

"First..." Zahra stood up and went to Dunya. "Are you all right?" she asked. She inspected Dunya's head and murmured, "Just a bruise, nothing more."

Dunya shuddered, fighting the urge to cry. As the night went on, Dunya recovered from her fear, bit by bit.

The tale of Yasmeen was a bawdy story with many euphemisms that Dunya did not understand, though the Sultan laughed until he drooled. When Yasmeen's story came to its absurd conclusion (according to Dunya), Zahra began another tale.

This one was about a king who liked to disguise his royal station and wander among the people of his city. He was visiting the poorestsection—the Jewish quarter—when he heard a song of joy coming from a humble shack. Inside he found a shoemaker named Lironi, whose faith and joy in her God were great, and who trusted in her God to carry her day by day—

"Why is it always a woman?" the Sultan asked peevishly. "Your stories are always about women. Why can't you tell a story about a man, for once? Or can't you think of someone unlike yourself for a full minute?"

"But this story does have a man in it," Zahra explained, so meek and mild. "It has the King."

The Sultan continued to argue, before eventually capitulating and letting her resume her story, but Dunya, sitting to one side with a pastry in her hands, had an idea.

As dawn began to stain the eastern horizon, the Sultan waved a hand and yawned. "I can't stay awake any longer," he said to Zahra. "You're pardoned for the day—I need to sleep."

As he stretched out on the bed, Dunya got to her feet.
She cleared her throat. "Zahra?" "Yes?" Zahra
turned to her.

"May I ask a favor of you?"

"Of course."

"Show me the city."

"I beg your pardon?"

Dunya glanced at the sleeping Sultan. Zahra understood at once, and the two of them went out to the balcony. "I've been thinking about this all night," Dunya said. "I want to go into the city, like the King in your story. I'm scared, but—I've wondered about it all my life. Would you come with me? You know the city much better than I do, I'm sure."

"I suppose I do," Zahra covered her mouth with her fingers, thinking. "But I cannot follow you. I have to stay here."

"But –"

"I have to stay here."

"But you have magic," Dunya insisted in a whisper.

"I will not be moved on this," Zahra said. "But I have loaned you a scarf that may help. And—here."

Zahra stepped behind Dunya. She laid one hand on Dunya's shoulder, and with the other she began to point out districts of the city, which became clearer as the sky brightened.

"Do you see the treetops on that boulevard? That is the Street of Sycamores, where the Viziers and other wealthy citizens live. Your father's house is there. On the other side of that street is the banking district. Now, if we move north —you see a bit of the old city wall there—there are markets close by the Palace walls and the river. Weaver's street— which you can find by its smell—and beyond that, the Demon's Market."

Dunya turned her head to look at Zahra, who said, "It's not as frightening as it sounds, although it does have its share of dangers. The wares there are tempting, but the prices are often steep. Do you understand?"

"Yes."

Dunya listened closely as Zahra continued to point out districts in the city, even the ones that were blocked by the Palace itself. The pieces formed a tenuous whole in Dunya's mind, a map that she couldn't wait to fill in.

Part Two

The Miserable Djinni

It was a week later, and Dunya had not yet brought her plan to fruition. Zahra's tale had branched out into several smaller tales within the tale—for instance, she was about to share a soldier's story when a messenger came to the door.

"Your Majesty, there is a courier sent here from Munir. Urgent news about the border skirmishes."

The Sultan swore by three prophets and four bodily functions and set off to meet the courier. After he had left, the messenger remained in the doorway, bowing towards the Sultan, and then he abruptly straightened up, adjusted his turban, and said, "Which of you ladies is Dunya, daughter of Shareef?"

Zahra looked her way. Dunya got to her feet. "I am," she said.

"The courier brought this and said I was to deliver it to you, personally, without the Sultan's knowing," said the messenger. He presented a wrapped packet with a small scroll. "I would suggest you open it soon."

"Oh. Thank you…You'll be wanting a tip?" Dunya had no jewelry on her, and if this gift came from who she thought it came from, nothing she had would be sufficient payment…

Zahra removed one of her gold bangles and gave it to the messenger, who bowed, said, "Your loyal servant, ladies," and quietly waited.

Dunya unfolded the letter first. It read:

"Dunya, daughter of Shareef and explorer of bookshelves,

I have prayed that the message I received from your father was in jest, or untrue, or that I had mistaken it somehow. Your father wrote to me some four weeks ago, saying that he had married you to the Sultan. I only received the message now, and it will take another two weeks for this letter to reach you.

Please send word back with my messenger, whether to tell me if this news is true or false, but most important, to tell me if you can bear the way you are living, if indeed living you still are when you receive this (I pray).

What I am giving you should be kept secret. It is a good luck charm and I have had it since I was a little boy. I like to think that it has protected me and I hope that it shall protect you.

May God's grace be with you,

Munir, son of Junayd"

Dunya unwrapped the package. She was expecting something exotic, something obviously powerful and impressive, and was surprised to find a long chain with a simple, flat pendant of hammered bronze, shaped like a bird in flight.

"This is his good luck charm?" she asked out loud.

"He sent you a good luck charm?" Zahra asked. "May I see it?"

Dunya held it out to her. "It's not what I was expecting. He says he has had it since he was a child." Dunya had few possessions of her own—her father's house had provided all the necessities, but she was not, by nature, given to hoarding sentimental items. "Probably he has a whole room full of them."

"I do not think so," said Zahra. "He brought it with him all the way to the borderlands. Perhaps it means a great deal to him."

That phrase struck in Dunya's mind like a match. "You think so?" she asked, taking it back from Zahra's hand. "Why would he give me something that's so important?"

"I have an answer for you. I advise that you hide that charm from the Sultan." She hurriedly unspooled the chain, set it around her neck, and tucked the bird between the layers of her robes.

"But what's your answer?" Dunya whispered.

"First, dear, the messenger."

"Oh, yes." Dunya turned to the messenger. "Tell Munir…" she hesitated and looked at Zahra. "Tell Munir that I can bear the way that I'm living now. That I have a…a friend, I guess."

The messenger acknowledged this and quickly left. Zahra then turned to Dunya and said, "That answer will do for now. But it will not allay Munir's fear."

Dunya paused. "Munir is afraid…of what?"

"I should say of whom."

"Of the Sultan? His cousin?"

Zahra nodded. "And afraid for…" her last word was a whisper, and she completed her sentence by tapping Dunya on the forehead.

Afraid for me, Dunya thought. The idea was intriguing, and she was not sure if she believed it. "Well, that's very kind of him," was what she settled on saying. "But he needn't be afraid any longer. After all, you've eased the Sultan's madness."

"I have not," said Zahra, with a sudden sternness that made Dunya sit up. "Have you been too sleepy to hear the Sultan in the evening? Too tired to see him in the morning?" She leaned in close to Dunya, and her black eyes were arresting. "Think, little one."

"I'm not *that* little," Dunya protested. But she tried to think. "Every evening, the Sultan asks that you finish the story you started."

"He asks, does he?"

"No…he commands." Dunya's brow furrowed. "And every morning he's in a bad mood to hear the story unfinished. And he leaves…but he always commands that you stay here. And he reminds the guards to kill you if you leave the chamber…" She sighed and sagged onto the cushions. "He is still insane, then."

"For the time being, yes."

"He could kill you any day. He could kill me next."

"So Munir is quite right to be afraid for you."

"Zahra…" Dunya sat up again. "You knew that the Sultan was mad and murderous, did you not?"

"Most of the Kingdom knows it by now, little one."

"But you still came. Why? Why did you put yourself right into his path?"

Zahra opened her mouth, but hesitated. This in itself was so unusual that Dunya paid close attention when she did finally speak. "I have hope," she said. "It is a new emotion in my heart."

"You never hoped before?"

She closed her mouth tightly and shook her head, her eyes glittering. "Have I said too much? No. I have hope that my stories will help to calm the Sultan's heart. Teach him wisdom and goodness and repentance. To see through the eyes of others."

"But the Sultan is so stubborn…they might not do anything. He might kill you. And then…" Dunya closed her eyes. "And then I'm next. I'm next. I'm afraid, Zahra."

"Do not dwell on fear. How about your idea? I've sensed you coveting it the last few days.."

Dunya pulled a long lock of hair down over her shoulder. "I want to go out into Al-Rayyan. And see how other people live."

"My stories are having a good effect on you." Dunya opened her eyes and she saw Zahra smiling at her.

"But there are so many dangers there. Father always warned me…so easy to get lost, and never find my way home…"

"Dunya. You are a prudent and careful girl, but I say to you again, do not be afraid. Life is short, especially life married to our supreme Sultan. Do you want to live all your life behind walls?" When Dunya didn't answer, Zahra replied in a kinder tone, "If you would be advised by me, venture into Al-Rayyan. I showed you the city. It is waiting for you."

Footsteps sounded. The Sultan was approaching. Dunya clasped Zahra's hands and said, "I will follow your advice," before the Sultan returned and the story could continue.

The Palace collectively began to adjust to the new order —Zahra, the Sultana-for-now, and Dunya, the girl with uncertain rank. One day, Dunya returned from the library to find her clothes from her father's house, arrayed in a cedar chest, in her bedroom. She had been wearing castoffs from the harem, and it felt good to run her fingers over the materials that she knew.

The half-formed plan in her head began to take a firmer shape. The city beckoned.

On one bright, clear day, Dunya dressed and wrapped Zahra's blue scarf over her hair. She left the Sultan's suite. Her slippered feet padded past the gardens, past the harem, and to the throne room, where the Sultan met with supplicants.

Dunya paused, getting her bearings. A stray breeze tickled her cheek, and she gave a half-smile and followed it.

She followed the air currents and the light until she came to a great door. Guards were posted at either side, but they gave her no notice. She stepped closer, but they made no move to stop her. As simple as that, she crossed the first door.

Now she was on a promenade, wide enough for carriages and lined by cypress trees. The walls of the Palace lay ahead of her.

Dunya started to run—remembering that running wouldn't be seemly for a young lady—then remembering that no one took notice of her under the cover of magic. She darted forward. She passed the first cypress tree, and stopped to run her hands along its fragrant needles. It felt rough, a little sticky, and very real.

She felt a new breeze, and all of a sudden, Dunya couldn't wait another moment to be out of the walls and into the city. She walked towards the Palace gate. It was made of some metal, green with age, and worked with patterns as delicate as lace. There was a door set into the gate's right hand side, and a guard by the door.

Dunya stopped here. With an eye on the guard, she pushed the door open. A new breeze met her. She took it as a good sign. She passed through the door and closed it behind her.

She was standing on a broad boulevard and could see many little streets winding off this one. Far ahead of her, the river glinted.

"Let's go there," she said to herself, and set off.

The streets were shadowed by tall houses on either side of the boulevard. As she progressed, the houses gave way to shops, and then to merchant's stalls. The smells on the air—food vendors, spices, —the horses of couriers - grew stronger. A passing herd of goats kicked up dirt, which made Dunya cough and rub her eyes.

She reached the river and stopped there. The play of light on the water caught her eye, but when someone bumped into her, she drew her outer robe about her more tightly and began to observe the crowd. Everyone was walking with purpose, a place to be, and they had to be there soon. It was very different from the relaxed saunter that most courtiers in the Palace affected.

She'd do her best to blend in, then. But in which direction to head? Arbitrarily, she went right.

She tried to remember the neighborhoods that Zahra had pointed out. She could still see the Palace walls between buildings, so she wasn't far at all. As long as she didn't get lost, she'd be fine.

"That's the weaver's street," she muttered under her breath, "and that, the food markets." Someone was roasting pine nuts. Her mouth watered, but she remembered she didn't have any coins. She'd have to get back to the Palace before too long. Just as well, she told herself. Just as well.

Archways of white stone or wood marked new neighborhoods. Washing lines crisscrossed between buildings, high above her head. Boats crowded the river. Striped awnings gleamed in the sunlight. Everywhere, there was activity and motion and so much light. It was a world away from the austere rooms and careful patterns of the Palace, or the stillness of her father's house. Dunya didn't know where to start—or even where to stop. Just don't lose

sight of the Palace, she thought.

She stopped before an archway. The lower half of the archway archway, was covered with dangling blue-eye medallions, to ward against evil. There was graffiti, some obscene, some warnings to stay away from other parts of town.

Zahra had called this part of town the Demon's Market. But other than the charms on the archway, it seemed like any other stretch of the city.

Dunya crossed under the archway. If there's the first sign of danger, she thought, I'll leave. Just turn around and return to the Palace. She proceeded swiftly, not making eye contact with anyone—and something to her right went thud. Dunya jumped, and was half-turned back when she saw the source of the noise. It was just a black cat, jumping from an awning.

"Scaredy-cat," Dunya muttered to herself.

That noise, she realized, had stood out because the rest of the street was so quiet. Even the merchants at their stands were talking amongst themselves, rather than boasting about their wares. There was only one other person on the street— a tall girl about Dunya's age, in a cinnamon-colored scarf. She slumped forward, towards an intersection and fountain. Dunya followed her—the girl looked ill, in need of help.

When the girl reached the rim of the fountain, she sank onto its edge, breathing heavily.

"Are you all right?" Dunya asked.

The girl looked up at her. She had strong features and a desolate expression. Flakes of ash clung to her hairline and eyelashes. "No," she said, "obviously not."

"You're sick," Dunya said. "Let me get help –"

"Nothing can help me." The girl's fist clenched over the rim of the fountain. Ash shook from her sleeve.

"Of course something can," Dunya said. She knelt in front of the girl. "I'm Dunya. What's your name?"

"Upalu," said the girl with the cinnamon-colored scarf. "There's too much wrong. Just leave me be."

"What's wrong?"

"Can't you feel it?" Upalu asked. "The city is sick."

"Sick?"

Upalu gestured with one hand towards the empty street. "Everyone here knows it. That's why they left or are barricading themselves inside."

"I don't know it."

Upalu looked at her. Her eyes were a surprisingly light hazel, almost gold. "You're human," she said.

"Er…yes, I am."

"Humans are no good at sensing things. Promisebreakers. Heartbreakers. Leave me be."

She isn't human, Dunya thought. That doesn't matter. "Let me fetch a doctor."

"I don't need a doctor."

"What do you need then?"

Upalu's breath hitched. "Nothing you can help me with."

"Try me."

"I need…my heart…damnation, it sounds so stupid." She made a fist over her heart. Her clenched hand was shedding flakes of ash and embers.

"What are you, if you're not human?" Dunya asked. "I'm sorry if I'm rude…"

"I'm a djinn," said Upalu. "The most worthless specimen of djinn. My magic has dried up. One more disaster for this city."

Djinn. Dunya's mind raced. Made from the blood of Allah. Fire spirits. The ash… "You're dying," she said, almost a whisper.

"That's a risk of my kind," Upalu said. Now that Dunya knew what to look for, the djinn seemed to be flaking away before her very eyes. She looked bloodless, starved. "Get your heart broken, your fire dies, your magic dies, you die." "Get away from the water." Dunya got to her feet.

"You trying to save me, or something?" Upalu snorted. "Let me guess, you're a good fairy here to reverse my love fortune. Try someone else."

"No…but I know a kitchen, with enormous fireplaces. Surely the fire there could help…you…"

Upalu looked at her, eyes narrowed. Then she studied Dunya's hands.

"What?" Dunya asked.

"You don't work in a kitchen."

"I work in the Palace," Dunya said.

"I wouldn't go there for a shipful of cedarwood. The Palace is too dangerous."

"I've survived it, and I'm not special at all," Dunya said. "You don't have to stay long, but come with me. Don't give up. Please."

Upalu stared blankly at the ground.

"Please," Dunya said.

Finally, Upalu heaved a sigh. "I've already left her behind. Why not. Fine."

She got to her feet. Dunya said, "This way," and Upalu followed without protest. The djinn only halted when they reached the archway of the Demon's Market.

"It's alright," Dunya said to her. "I know, it can be scary."

"What? Oh, no, I was going to say, if we're going to the Palace, there's a better route."

Upalu took the lead with no fanfare. The silence began to get to Dunya. She coughed and said, "This area of town seems really quiet."

"Most people have left."

"By people, you mean…" Dunya almost said demons, but politeness stopped her. You never knew…

"Ifrits, harpies, djinni, rusalka from up north, anyone passing through…you know, people."

"Oh. I'm sorry…"

Upalu snorted. Dunya asked, "Why have the people left?"

"Because the omens are bad. Magic is blighted—not just in me, but in lots of people. This city isn't healthy anymore.

"You have to have a clue, even if you are just a human."

"When did it start?"

"Around the time that the Sultana died. The first one, I should say."

After a pause, Dunya asked, "Where did it start?" afraid that she already knew the answer.

Upalu gave her a disbelieving look. "In the Palace. Where else?"

Now it was Dunya's turn to be silent and think on what she was hearing. Upalu asked, "Did you leave by the main gate, or one of the kitchen gates?"

"Um, the main gate." At that, Upalu turned right. The main gate came into sight, with guards posted before it.

"I can get past them," Dunya said, fingering her blue scarf, "but you…" She looked up. Upalu shrugged, as if she didn't particularly care what happened to her.

"Let's just try," Dunya said. She strode towards the gates and heard Upalu's footsteps, very quiet, behind her. Dunya did not make eye contact with the guards, but walked forward, and soon she stood in the shadows of the cypress trees again. Upalu stopped beside her.

"It worked!" Dunya whispered.

"Kind of lazy security you guys have here," Upalu remarked.

"Don't chide them. It's some magic," Dunya said.

It turned out that the Palace was larger than Dunya had anticipated. But, by her estimation, they only got lost once
—when they found themselves in the workshops. Fortunately, the people in the dye works took notice of Dunya when she spoke to them, and pointed out the way to the kitchens.

On the way to the kitchens, Dunya noticed that Upalu looked less and less well. Was that smoke coming off of her?
"We're almost there," Dunya said to her.

"Worry about yourself," Upalu said. "I'll worry about me."

The kitchens had wide wooden doors, and they were now propped wide open to let the heat out. People were hurrying in and out, and loud voices sounded from inside.

"Maybe we should wait until it's quiet…" Dunya said— only to watch Upalu vanish into the hustle.—"Oh, no," Dunya grumbled as she followed Upalu in.

The kitchen was overwhelming—like all the sensations that Dunya had glimpsed in the city, packed into one large room. The smells, the noise, the people…it was all Dunya could do to keep her head and scan the room for a cinnamon-colored scarf.

There—by the fireplace, along the far wall. Dunya ran towards it. Upalu walked towards the fireplace—and stopped short. Dunya caught up with her.

"There," she said. "I told you it was a large fireplace."

"I don't know if it will work," said Upalu. "But…" She glanced at Dunya, "thank you for bringing me here. Thank you for trying."

"You are welcome. Um…what do you do now?"

"I can't stay in this form," Upalu said with a shrug. When her shoulders fell, she became insubstantial—colorless—in a moment, Upalu became a column of smoke, which sank into the fireplace. Were the embers glowing more brightly? Was the fire different, now that a djinn dwelt there?

Dunya stood, watching the flames, trying to spot a difference, until someone bumped into her and said, "There's no place in this kitchen for sightseers!"

Dunya got out of his way and found a place to sit, close to the fire. She checked the sunlight—the day was still young. She waited, watching the activity of the kitchen. She watched as vast quantities of food were prepared and sent out— some to Palace workers, some to Viziers and their entourages, and some, Dunya imagined, to the Sultan himself. The kitchen staff was resting after lunch, and Dunya's stomach was growling, by the time she spoke.

"I hope you like it here," she said.

"I'm very tired," came a whisper from the fire. Dunya looked. A vaguely human-shaped form was visible in the licks of flame. "Thank you for bringing me here. Now you can leave."

"I won't. I want to know your story."

"Well, I don't feel like sharing. Just…just go." The fire seemed to give a little huff, and the flames fell back into being regular flames. Dunya pulled down her blue scarf. She approached a chef, took a meat pie to eat, and settled by the fire again.

She had finished her meat pie and was back to watching the flames. In time, the djinn's figure became visible again.

"Why are you still here?" the djinn asked.

"I want to make sure you're not lonely."

"My heart is broken. Of course I'm lonely."

"Who broke your heart?"

"A human girl. Woman, rather."

"I'm very sorry to hear that."

"And now a human girl is here to rescue me. This is the contract up on its head."

"What contract?"

Upalu rolled her head back and heaved a sigh—a puff of smoke went up the chimney. "Djinni are siblings to humans. Humans are made of earth, djinni are made of fire, and Allah granted us both free will, to make of our lives what we choose. Well, it is also proper for a djinn to make a home in a vessel, be it of clay, or metal, or glass. And a djinn will wait in that vessel, and trust in God's plan to take us to where we should be. And...a human will find the djinn."

She paused a long time, and Dunya asked her to go on.

"It's a stupid story. It's a very old story. I loved, I lost. One of the oldest stories that there is. And when my wishes dried up, I was dismissed—with all due politeness, of course —and that is where you found me."

"That's awful." Upalu turned away from Dunya, and the human girl said, "I know what it is like to be cast aside— given up—treated as worthless. My father gave me...well, gave me in service to the Palace, you might say, as a show of good faith. That's how Shirin put it."

"Who is Shirin?"

"A friend of mine. She's dead now. I would be dead, too..." Dunya swallowed. Even now, her voice trembled, "if it weren't for Zahra."

"Who is Zahra?"

"I... I don't know where she came from. She has the title of Sultana."

"Oh. A mortal, then."

Dunya looked sidelong at Upalu. She was, suddenly, not sure. But Upalu's mind had turned back to her own troubles, and she sighed deeply and said, "You want to hear my story? Here it is. God's will put me in the hands of a poor girl. Djinn-wishes should balance the world—elevate the lowly, cast down the mighty. You know—good reversals, turnabouts."

"And what wishes were asked of you?"

Upalu shrugged. "Nothing too fancy. The girl asked for a home for her family. A workshop for her art. A fountain inlaid with blue tiles in the shapes of lotuses. I could have given her the stars! And I let myself be charmed by her humility. I fell in love...and I thought she was my friend, but she said she could never love a djinni. Something—not human." Upalu's voice broke. "She said she didn't want to see me ever again." The djinni seemed to collapse into nothing but a pile of embers. "How could she? How could she do that to me?"

"I'm sorry." That phrase began to sound inadequate the more Dunya said it. "But...I'm sure you'll feel better soon."

That earned her a glare that was all the more potent coming from eyes of fire. "Is that all you can think to say?"

"I'm sorry, I don't have much experience with...affairs of the heart?"

Upalu actually laughed that. "I can tell."

"But I've heard many stories...Listen, this Palace, there are many wonders. I heard of a magic carpet in the basement...there' s a tree whose leaves sing lullabies to… um, itself…" Dunya's voice trailed off. Upalu was staring at her. "What I mean to say is, maybe you'll find healing here. Maybe you just need a change of scenery. Anyway, I'll look after you."

Upalu nodded. She seemed to curl up some in the fire. "Very good. I feel protected already. Now…please, leave me alone."

Dunya got up, wished peace upon the djinn, and left. But she thought about Upalu often for the rest of the day, and resolved to visit her tomorrow.

Dunya went upstairs, to her private chamber adjoining the Sultan's. There, she prayed.

When she finished praying, she sat in still contemplation for a moment, going over everything that had happened that day. One venture outside the Palace walls had brought one stray djinni into the Palace household. And until today, Dunya hadn't been sure that djinn even existed!

And if one djinni existed…

Dunya replaced her veils and marched into the Sultan's bedchamber. Zahra was waiting there, as always. "I know what you are!" Dunya announced.

Zahra looked up from her scroll. "Yes?"

"You are not a human. You are a djinni! You have powers beyond the ken of mortals!" Dunya threw her arms wide. "It must be magic. You can make people forget things!"

Zahra, instead of swooning or admitting defeat, simply chuckled. "Silly child," she said. "The Sultan, too, has power. Is he also a djinn?"

"No, of course not. He's –"

"People do his bidding. He can order life, death, festivals —the entire course of this city rests in his hand. The Sultan can also make people forget things. Have you noticed that, since you came to the Palace, not one person has spoken the name of his first Sultana?" Zahra asked. "Is this not power?"

Dunya waved a hand. "That's just obedience. You have real magic!"

Zahra shook her head. "I am what I am. Nothing more than that."

Dunya slumped. "But why do you have power, then?"

"Power is the ability to see ahead," Zahra said to her. "Silly child. You still have so much to learn."

Dunya tried to come up with a witty rejoinder, failed, and sighed deeply.

"What is the matter?"

"Why does love hurt people so much? Why do people love those who don't love them back?"

Zahra spread her hands wide. "Ah, you've asked a question I cannot answer, except…"

"Yes?"

"Life isn't fair."

Dunya punched at a pillow. "That's not an answer!"

"We could have a philosophical discussion all through the night, if you would rather. Shall I order coffee?"

"Yes!— no…" Dunya turned, hearing the Sultan's footsteps coming down the hall. "You have to tell your stories tonight. But…just one question."

"Yes?"

"Do you love the Sultan?"

Zahra gave Dunya a very cool, detached look. "I try," was all she said, just as the Sultan entered.

The Sultan strode into the bedroom. Unwinding his red silk turban, he said, "Now you will continue the story, wife of mine. And do not forget the djinni of the pot of rouge! I like that character. He makes me laugh."

"I forget no one," Zahra promised him, and whatever face she had presented to Dunya a moment ago was gone. Now she was as smooth and meek as ever, only appearing to come to life when she began to unspool another wonderful story, thrilling and chilling by turns.

Dunya curled herself on the pillow, half-listening, thinking of djinn, strange storytellers who appeared in the night, and the young man on the border who had sent her a good luck charm—one which had, by all appearances, worked.

Two weeks passed by. Some days Dunya visited Upalu in the kitchen, and they talked. Over a piled plate of food, the djinni would tell Dunya a little more of her history. Sometimes when Upalu laughed, Dunya was sure she had done a good thing bringing her to the Palace. Other times…

"Wait, you mean–I thought that the talk about the Sultan was just rumors," Upalu said when Dunya had finished telling her story. "I thought that the stories about the Sultan having killed ninety-eight women were–were

rumor, nothing else! Exaggeration!"

"I believe what Morgiana and Shirin told me, and they said ninety-eight."

"And you are alive right now just because he–this wild Sultan–is interested enough in Zahra's stories to keep her alive?"

"Yes."

"She could have a sore throat tonight and be dead by tomorrow morning."

"Yes…yes, I never thought about that, but it's true."

"She could run out of stories."

"She hasn't yet. She never even hesitates– except when it's more dramatic to pause, of course."

"Aren't you afraid of her running out of stories?"

Dunya didn't answer for a moment. "I am."

"How do you even live like that?"

"I don't think about it too hard…" Dunya offered, trailing off.

Upalu gave a half-shrug and took another handful of food. "I guess a body can get used to just about anything, then. I thought that only djinn were that resilient."

Resilient. No one had ever applied that word to Dunya before. "Yes…I suppose so."

Then Dunya turned the conversation around. "And how are you? Is your magic coming back yet?"

"It's not as simple as that," Upalu replied, a bit haughtily. "And there's…there's something about this Palace. My magic feels weaker here."

"You're not fully recovered, that's all," Dunya assured her.

"I don't think that's it." On other days, Dunya went out into the city itself. She wore Zahra's headscarf, and no one saw or stopped her. She always found her way home and traveled safely.

During her visits, Dunya had to learn to navigate the crowds. She had never been among so many people in her life, of all stations, sizes, and states of personal cleanliness. It took gumption to elbow one's way through the crowd, and wits to navigate the best path, from one moment to another. But gumption could be grown and wits could be sharpened, and Dunya did both to navigate the thick market crowds that sprung up on either side of the Palace and along the river.

The river was Dunya's first true destination within the city. The colorful boats crowded the water, and people crowded the wharfs—whether they were merchants doing trade, sailors taking a chance to rest, or beggars bothering for a bit of coin. They, too, were invisible, Dunya noticed; all they had to do was hold out a bowl and eyes would flit right past them.

The next time she visited the old city, Dunya saw the beggars arranged carefully on the steps of the mosques. When a wealthy man would leave his Friday prayers, he would seek out one particular beggar, almost like a friend, and pass a few coins to him and ask after his welfare. This seemed better, but the system in place was clearly built for one rich man or family to one beggar. Dunya couldn't make sense of it.

The old city was dizzying just to walk in. Conversations passed between buildings over Dunya's head as gossips hung out their laundry. Musicians played for coins, smiling at their own tunes. There was so much life, so many people around.

Across the river there was the theater district, where the shops were filled with masks and coffee wafted out from restaurants. Dunya could hear debates inside—the people sounded very passionate. There were fewer musicians here and more storytellers—but Dunya felt a surge of pity for them, because none of them were Zahra. And Dunya would pinch her headscarf a little closer over her hair and look ahead to when she would reach the Palace safely—and she always reached it safely.

The blessing–or magic–or whatever it was, of passing unseen and finding her way home, turned upside-down the order of Dunya's world. While she passed through the city, unseen, the people of Al-Rayyan and the stones around her seemed to melt into a dream, interesting but without risk. In contrast, the stories that Zahra told, though they danced between Dunya's ears, seemed far more tangible and meaningful. In the city, things just happened. In the stories, there was order; the story might open new tales within itself, but she could trust that Zahra always had the kernel of it in hand, like an arrow in a bow's embrace.

In between her dreamlike life by day and the stories by night, Dunya knew that it would soon be time for the Sultan's birthday celebration. And she heard over a well in the Old Town–Munir would ride into the city to visit.

The day before the Sultan's birthday, Munir and his retinue rode into the Palace at dawn. And Dunya, who hadn't gone to sleep yet, watched them enter and then crept into the kitchen. She stirred Upalu awake by poking her with a stick.

"Ow! What is it?" asked Upalu.

"A wish of mine came true," Dunya told her. "Someone I wanted to see has come back to the Palace."

"I had nothing to do with it," Upalu grumbled.

"You didn't? Are you sure? No matter, I wanted to share with someone." Dunya hugged herself. "I'm so happy!"

Upalu rolled her eyes. "I'm going back to sleep, and I suggest you do the same."

Going to sleep was a fine idea, thought Dunya, as she tiptoed out of the kitchen. But outside the door, she met a familiar, stocky figure–Hussein, Munir's companion.

"What are you doing here?" he asked. Then, before she could answer, said, "No matter. Captain Munir would like to see you. I was asked to escort you to the Lotus Garden. That is, if her highness wishes. Those were his precise words."

Dunya wanted to go with him, and almost said so, but an enormous yawn cut off her words.

Hussein gave her a companionable grin. "A long night? I've been there." As Dunya weighed her desire for sleep versus her desire to see Munir again, right now, Hussein added, "Munir added that he wanted to meet as long as the Sultan is sleeping. Which is…"

"I'll come now," Dunya said.

As Hussein escorted her to the garden, he said to her, "A word of advice, just because the Sultan is asleep doesn't mean his eyes are closed. Do you understand?

"Whatever you and Munir say to each other, you must also look the very picture of brother-and-sisterly chastity. Because there will be people watching, eager to twist even the most innocent of gestures into some kind of scandal."

"Oh, that, I know that much. I am the daughter of the Grand Vizier, you know" Dunya said, as Hussein left her pass through a door.

Even exhausted, Dunya could see how beautiful the Lotus Garden was. Pools displayed water lilies of over a dozen varieties. Gardeners were already at work, and there were a few of the court's early risers strolling among the flowers. The sky was the cool lavender before dawn, and the air was already growing warm.

Munir was easy to spot even at a distance. His lanky frame was pacing back and forth between two pools. When he caught sight of Dunya, he smiled.

"There you are!" He bowed to her, his hands open. "Your highness…"

Dunya ran to him and stopped shy of touching him. "Don't call me that. It's good to see you."

She felt his surprise and tension, and then he relaxed. "It's good to see you, too. When I heard you were to be married to Sayyid…" He gently touched her arm and looked down into her face, "I feared for the worst."

"So did I," she said. "Morgiana died, and Shirin. They became my friends, and then…" She choked up and rubbed hard at her face. "I shouldn't cry! I'm just tired."

"I cried when I heard about them," he told her softly. "I don't understand what's happened. I thought you were to be married to the Sultan. I have seen the scroll that lists your name. But here you are, alive–and no one speaks of you except as the Princess of the second rank." He eyed her. "Who do you say that you are?"

"I am…" She took a deep breath. "I am the Sultana. Though I do not like it."

"Sayyid–has he touched you? Hurt you?"

"No. He barely sees me."

"You are blessed," Munir said, with a sigh. "I am so relieved to hear that. Is his madness lifted, then?"

"I do not think so. I think he is just distracted."

"Distracted? By what?"

"By Zahra"

"Zahra. I've heard that name. The court is full of speculation. They say she never leaves the Sultan's chambers. Is that true?"

"Zahra—" she began, and then bit her tongue. It was all so strange, and with Hussein's warning and all, maybe this wasn't the place or time. How well did she know Munir?

"Zahra is reclusive," she said, at last.

Munir nodded. She couldn't imagine he was satisfied with that answer, but he seemed to understand that there was a secret.

"How does she treat you?" he asked.

"What does that matter?"

"You are her rival."

"She treats me very kindly. She doesn't seem to bear me any ill will. And she tells the most wonderful stories."

Munir nodded, but didn't ask anything more. Dunya waited, then asked, "How long are you staying? In the Palace?"

"I'm not sure. I can't stay here long."

Dunya's face fell. "Oh.

"I'm sorry to sadden you, little bird. Say...did you receive the locket I sent you?"

She was still wearing it around her neck. She held it out for him to see.

"It seems to be doing you good! I'm glad to see that."

"I'm still alive," Dunya said drily. She looked up at him, and didn't think to hide how happy she was to see him—right up until she yawned. "I'm sorry," she ducked her head. "That was rude."

"You didn't sleep well?"

"I didn't go to sleep." Dunya yawned again, and pinched her cheek to try and stay awake. "How goes the fighting on the border?"

"Never mind that. I think it's time for you to go to bed, young Princess."

"But we haven't even begun to talk!" Dunya yawned again. Munir glanced over his shoulder, at anyone within earshot. "I will see you again soon, at the Sultan's birthday celebration." He did a decent job disguising his wince.

"Yes…" Dunya studied him. His long features were becoming clearer as the daylight gathered. He looked tired, too, like a hounded thing. She wanted to reach for his hand, but people were watching. Her heart thudded in her ears, and she tried to focus.

Her heart thudded a little louder. "Yes. Is it lonely, out in camp?"

He opened his mouth, glanced over his shoulder again, and then said diplomatically, "It's different than the company you find in the Palace." His eyes met hers. "Don't worry about me."

She didn't look away. She had his full attention. Her cheeks grew warm. "But," she managed to say, "I do worry about you."

His mouth quirked to one side in a wry smile. As he was about to say something, a noise interrupted—a gardener's tool falling to the tile. Munir seemed to remember where he was. "Your concern speaks well of you," he said, with a courteous nod. "I thank you."

Dunya didn't know what to say—she tried to imagine what First Wife Noora might do—and she curtsied. She yawned again. "I'm sorry," she said, looking down at her feet. "I should go and rest." When she glanced up at him, he was suppressing another smile. Was he laughing at her?

"Go and rest, Princess Dunya," he said. "We will speak again soon."

This interplay between courtesy and sincerity was spinning her head. She curtsied, said, "Good morning," and turned away.

"Good morning," she heard him call as she left the Lotus Gardens. She could almost feel the watchful eyes of everyone else slipping away and off of her. But it was nice, to have been noticed for a little while. And how nice it would be, to correspond with him by letter. It would make up for the brevity of their conversations.

She would really have to thank Upalu again.

The River Spirit and Her Grief

`The day of the Sultan's birthday arrived. While the Palace bustled with activity for the evening celebrations, the Sultan was quiet. He took himself to a high balcony to watch the guests arrive, and Dunya followed him there. She thought that she had been unnoticed, as usual, until she heard him say, "Sister-in-law. You're there, aren't you?" "Y-yes, sir," Dunya replied and started to shiver.

"Come over here and look over my shoulder. Or by my elbow," he added, with a glance at Dunya's height. Outside the Palace gates, there were sedans and litters and grand carriages, awaiting the trumpet call and the gates pulling open. Even up here, Dunya's ears caught the whinny of horses and the faint chatter of the guests.

"How do they do it?" said the Sultan. "How does anyone find meaning in their petty little lives?" He lifted his hand and pointed to one person—a distant dot—after another— after another. "He will die. And he will die. And he will die. How do they stomach that reality? Why do they bother going on?"

"Sire?" she asked in a small voice. "Are you…are you happy?"

"Happy?" the Sultan repeated. "I'm the happiest man I know. I'm the only soul that doesn't have to pretend."

He fell silent. Then he sighed. "Might as well get this over with." And he turned around and left Dunya alone on the balcony.

When she returned to the main room, a messenger was waiting for her. He carried a short note, which read, "If you would meet me in the library before I leave, I would be very grateful – Munir." There was a postscript: "The geography shelf."

Zahra presided over the feast, as regal a Queen as any could wish to find. The Viziers presented their gifts to the Sultan. Each gift was costly and laden with meaning of some kind. Zahra explained these meanings to Dunya in a patient, steady whisper.

Munir, for his gift, presented a year-old colt with all the makings of a great stallion.

He left early, claiming he needed his sleep before an early departure tomorrow.

Dunya waited a few minutes and then left herself, murmuring that she wasn't feeling well. As soon as she was out of sight of the banquet hall, she hurried to the library. The geography shelf was easy to find—she knew where the large globe showing the known world rested, along with slanted tables for reading or drawing more maps. Munir was waiting for her there.

"Captain," she said, coming to a halt and curtsying.

He sketched a bow in response. "Dunya," he said, "I wanted to see you before I left."

"Thank you for your message."

His smile in return was sheepish. "I—if it is not too much to ask—I would like it if you wrote to me."

Dunya's heart raced. She smiled and said, "Yes, I would be happy to write to you. By, —um, —by Palace courier, I suppose."

"Yes."

"And I could tell you Zahra's stories. They're so good."

"Yes, Zahra…" He lowered his voice. "Does she really just… tell stories? And that's kept her alive?"

"Yes." Dunya felt a swell of pride in Zahra's accomplishment.

"Incredible. Yes, I'd like to know what stories she tells that have saved her head. And I really want to hear from you, and know you are alright."

A blush crept from Dunya's neck and started to spread over her face. She hoped the light was too dim to see it, knew that it was not. "You're very kind," she said.

"Your sister," Munir said, "is remarkable."

Dunya automatically wanted to say, She's not my sister, but something stopped her. Walls had ears. Anyone could be listening on the other side of the stacks. If Zahra's spell was broken, would her life be forfeit? This was dangerous knowledge. And so, she didn't interrupt Munir, who went on,

"As are you."

"Thank you," Dunya said, her blush flaring up again.

Behind him, a lieutenant whispered to Munir. H halfturned, said, "I hear you," and turned back to her. "I have to go," he said. "Write to me, please."

"I will."

He took her hands—his were callused and warm—and bowed over them and said, "God be with you," then he was gone.

By the time Dunya made it back her chambers, dawn was already staining the horizon, but still the Sultan insisted that Zahra continue the story she had begun the previous night. Dunya could not stay awake for this; she tottered to her own small bedchamber and fell asleep there.

She had a very strange dream.

She dreamed that she was sinking slowly through the rooms of the Palace, from the royal bedchambers, to the offices of Viziers, to the receiving rooms, to the Palace baths…and down further than that, sinking through stone. Throughout her descent she could hear someone sobbing, a wretched, broken sound, interrupted by splashes.

She dreamed, she sensed a lake, a part of the river, flowing powerfully under the Palace, sealed in total darkness, but going towards the light. And something else…

Dunya's heart raced. There was a woman trapped in the river! She bobbed in the water and threw her head back for huge, howling sobs.

Dunya reached out. "Take my hand!"

The woman didn't seem to hear her at all. Instead she submerged herself, and underwater she screamed so loudly and so terribly that Dunya woke up.

It was still early morning, and Dunya's thoughts were all scattered.

She crept into the Sultan's bedroom. The Sultan and Zahra were lying side-by-side in bed, but Zahra was awake and staring at Dunya curiously. She held a finger to her lips and slipped out of bed, still wearing her nightclothes, which were all black. Dunya wondered if everything Zahra owned was black, as Zahra led her out onto the balcony. "What is it?" Zahra asked. "You seem troubled." Dunya told her about the dream.

"Zahra," she said when she had finished, "What is there beneath this castle?"

"An underground lake—not a large one—from the bend in our river."

"No one could live there, could they?"

"I think any human would drown in moments."

"I dreamed of someone there. She was sobbing so much. Someone ought to go help her."

"Sshh, sshh." Zahra hugged her and stroked her hair. "It was only a dream, little sister."

"It didn't feel like other dream I've had. It felt like...I don't know what it felt like. But what if it was true?"

"Just let your dreams be dreams."

"Can't a dream be real?"

"Dunya, do you know how Al-Rayyan was founded?"

"I know about the Sultan Rifat and how he built the Palace. My grandmother told me."

"Very good. But the city was here before that. Back then it was only a collection of tents, but the river spirit had struck a bargain. Do you want to hear this story?"

"I always want to hear your stories, Zahra. They're wonderful."

Zahra smiled at her and told the tale of the river spirit'sgrief while the morning sun rose and the air grew warm. When she was finished, Dunya looked over her shoulder, into the quiet bedroom.

"That was a good story. But I just wondered, what if the Sultan heard you talking and grew jealous?"

"He is my husband, but he has no claim on my words," Zahra answered. "If he wants to hear the story, he can always ask."

Dunya was silent a long time. Zahra, as always, did not press or leave. She just stayed there, watching the sunrise with Dunya.

"Can a dream be dangerous?"

"If one spends too long in it, yes," was Zahra's answer.

"And then one's mind would grow ill," Dunya said.

"What are you thinking?"

"I'm thinking of Sultan Sayyid." Dunya sighed. "I am so tired of living like this, afraid of every sunrise, afraid it will be your last—or mine."

"And what would you do, then?"

Dunya couldn't answer. Finally, she said, "I think you've done more than your fair share of helping. It's time that I helped, too."

Dunya hurried to the kitchen as soon as she dressed. She had a wish for Upalu to grant.

She was surprised to see the kitchen far more crowded than usual. Aynabat and the other chefs were yelling for order, but many servants—more than worked in the kitchens—were crowding around the great fireplace, the one where Upalu lived. Some were on hands and knees before the hearth, others were standing at a distance and throwing salt and spices towards the flames.

"Please, a wish!"

"Grant me a wish!"

"No, my family needs this wish, listen to me!"

"No, me!"

Dunya stopped in her tracks and surveyed the scene with wide eyes. "Oh, no," she whispered. She was clutching her bird-shaped locket, and she felt it grow hot in her hands.

In a moment, it was too hot for her to hold.

A fierce whisper sounded as she let it go, "Get me out of here!"

Dunya obeyed, turning on her heels and running out of the kitchen, hearing people cry that the fire had died out, and what did that mean?

She hesitated in the hallway, unsure of where to go. Finally she ran to the east, out through the rose garden and into the empty tower of the harem. Wincing, she pulled the locket off from around her neck and dropped it onto the carpet. Upalu boiled up out of it, mercifully keeping herself a tall pillar of flame, not touching any of the flammable things in the room—and most of the things in the harem were flammable.

"What was that all about?" Dunya asked the djinni.

"I don't know, you tell me! How many people did you tell about me?"

"Maybe they worked it out for themselves? I did tell Zahra…"

Upalu rubbed her face hard, as molten-glass tears threatened to fall. "Humans are so silly. And so greedy. I can't stand it."

"I'm sorry," said Dunya. "This is all my fault. I should have found you somewhere safer to stay."

"Someplace to rest," said Upalu with a sigh.

There was a pause, and then Dunya said, "I'll take you out of the Palace. And you can go where you want. I just have one small wish."

"I can't grant it."

"A remedy to heal Sultan Sayyid's illness."

Upalu's flame dimmed. From a tall pillar she shrank and curled up on herself until she was about Dunya's own height. "What are you doing?" Dunya asked.

"That's a wish I cannot grant," said Upalu, shrinking in further, "except by advising you. Wait a moment."

There was a burst of light, and Upalu shaped herself again. She set down feet, not tongues of flame, onto the carpet, which hissed a little, but did not scorch. She shaped herself into her girl form again. "Don't expect too much," Upalu said, looming a little awkwardly over the girl, "but ask me your questions and I'll give you what answers I can. That's as close as I can come to granting your wish properly."

When Dunya's astonishment ebbed, she stumbled on her words and then said, "But you wanted to leave. I won't keep you from that."

"But first I will grant your wish. The worst thing about being mobbed…well…" She picked up the bird-shaped locket and held it out to Dunya, who took it with wrapped fingers, "…The worst thing, after being treated like a treasure to be stolen and abused…was that I could not grant a single wish. Not even the gentlest and best of them. Maybe you're right. Maybe I do need practice."

She glared at Dunya under thick brows. "But don't go gloating about being right."

Dunya invited Upalu to sit on the cushions of the harem, and for a moment Dunya was tempted to get out the chessboard. Dunya simply began by saying, "The Sultan's mind must have snapped. He is unreasonable, distrustful, short-tempered—he sees enemies everywhere, particularly in the women he is married to. I want to find out how I can undo this and restore him to sanity."

"Well…he is the Sultan. Seeing enemies everywhere might be sane, for him."

"But wanting to kill his wife, every sunrise?"

"Fair enough. … Did he ask you to seek out a remedy?"

"No."

"Does he know you're searching for a remedy?"

"No."

"The most important question—does he regret the way he is? Does he want to change?"

"I don't…think…so," Dunya answered. "But he must! So many lives depend on him."

"'But he must.' Oh, the wishes that have started with that phrase. I'm sorry, my friend, but when it comes to the mind, so often, one must wish to change in order to change."

"That's absurd!" Dunya burst out. "Why, I've—I've changed a great deal just in the past month, and I did not particularly want to."

"You're very philosophical, you know that?"

"I'm just contrary. That's what my grandmother said when I was naughty."

Upalu took Dunya's hands. "Small lady, I do not doubt that you've changed, but I think that was the natural result of challenges and adventures. But a person with a restful life must want change in themself before their spirit makes even the smallest transformation. I am sorry, but without the Sultan's willpower, anything you wish for, or buy from the Demon's Market will yield only puffs of smoke and deep regret."

"So that is the answer to my wish? Nothing will help, because the Sultan does not wish to change?"

"You could attempt a purchase," Upalu said, "But be warned. If someone seeks to change another against their will, that is always wicked magic. It corrupts the soul. The price is always high, and not paid in gold. Take that advice from me, if you would take nothing else."

This was a heavy consideration. Finally Dunya said, "I don't want to traffic in wicked magic."

"Then you have limited your choices," the djinni replied, "But I think you will not regret it."

"What about you?" Dunya asked. "At the height of your powers, could you heal the Su—my husband?" After a while, Upalu shook her head.

"Then I'll find another djinni, one who can. There must be one in the city."

"Few would come to the Palace," Upalu interrupted. "Djinn like myself prefer to work with the powerless. It is our delight to balance the scales of the world, not to give our power to those with power of their own. Besides, I do not think the Sultan is ill, to be healed."

"Then what is he?"

"I think you know. He is, quite simply, a very bad person."

Dunya sighed. "That is too simple an answer. It cannot be changed."

Upalu shrugged.

There were trumpets behind Upalu.

"What could that be?" Dunya asked.

"Not my problem," was the djinni's cheerful reply.

"Where will you go?"

Upalu looked around the empty harem "I think I will stay here." Upalu crossed the room to a metal brazier, which stood empty of kindling. "It's quiet. And no one lives here, do they?"

"Not anymore," Dunya said in a small voice.

"I'll stay here. I'll find fuel. You'd better go see what those trumpets are about."

"Very well," said Dunya. She got to her feet, and was surprised when Upalu enveloped her in a hug, feverish warm, but close. Dunya hadn't realized how starved she was for a little closeness and friendship.

"Go and see about those trumpets," said Upalu gruffly.

From outside they heard, "Announcement by order of the Sultan! Come all and hear!"

Dunya went, saying to herself, She'll leave eventually. Everyone leaves.

Sultan Sayyid was standing atop a balcony, with Zahra at his side. Courtiers and servants, paused in their work, looked up at him as he said, "Subjects! Shout the good news and dance in the streets, for my wife has promised me an heir!"

"What?" Dunya whispered.

Dunya hurried to the Sultan's chambers, where she found a crowd of people. Zahra was propped up on pillows, with doctors and attendants on either hand. She looked very satisfied with herself. At her feet there was an astrologer, explaining a cursory horoscope for the new heir. And by the window was the Sultan, pacing as usual, with his five

Viziers.

"Tomorrow, we shall go on a lion hunt," said the Sultan. "Pelts shall cover the cradle, and I– I could use the exercise," he added with a laugh. "See to it that my queen is conveyed in the proper style and comfort."

"Your queen?" asked the Vizier of Trade. "Surely she will rest in the Palace, in her condition."

"No," said the Sultan, with a glint in his eye. "She's a strong brood mare. She has promised me stories, and I will not leave those stories behind. She will attend on me, or else." He spotted Dunya. "Oh, and you can come, as well," he said to her. The Vziers turned to her in surprise.

She was just as surprised as they. It seemed a long while until the last doctor finally cleared out– it was late twilight by then. The Sultan was gone for a moment, and Dunya knelt by Zahra's side. As the woman sat up, Dunya asked her, "You're really going to have a child?" "I have promised, haven't I?" Zahra asked.

"But women can't promise that. Any number of things could go wrong."

"I know."

"How can you promise that? And, how did you even manage with the Sultan. He's so repulsive," Dunya shuddered.

"It is my duty as a good wife," said Zahra. "And you may trust me when I make a promise, little one. What's with that look?" she asked. Dunya was scowling at her.

"I don't understand you. I don't know what you want by being Sultana—and now you're going to have a child? I don't know what game you're playing. I don't even know who you are."

"I am who I am. And that is enough."

Dunya suddenly felt very small. And instead of feeling sad, she felt angry. She got up and stormed away to her own small chamber. Which, she realized, might no longer belong to her upon the arrival of Zahra's promised heir.

Dunya fumed as well as she could. After a time, she heard Zahra call for her. "It's time for the stories."

Zahra finished a story that night and began a new one about a man named Sinbad. Sinbad was a sailor who had been on seven voyages, and he (as Zahra told it) was relating his adventures to his doting but doubtful mother, Zummurud.

She listened to Zahra's stories faithfully that night, and the next, and the night after that, which Zahra told on the road, in a caravan fit for a king. Dunya admitted to herself that the stories were thrilling as anything, but something irritated her, and it only grew as the stories went on. For every adventure of Sinbad, there was a ship that foundered, or a companion carried off by a Roc or a manticore. The stories went on, and they arrived at the hunting grounds.

The first full day at the lion's grounds, the Sultan spent riding with his men. That night, he was so tired that he was nodding off, even during the story. Only Dunya was really awake to listen. That night, Sinbad's ship foundered for the seventh time, and for the seventh time, all souls aboard were drowned except for Sinbad himself, and Dunya clenched her fists and bit her tongue.

But Zahra stopped talking. She looked directly at Dunya and asked, "What is the matter?"

"I don't like Sinbad," Dunya began. "I don't like these stories."

"Why not?"

It took Dunya a moment to put into words precisely why. "Why is it," she asked, "That Sinbad survives every one of his journeys, but each one of his shipmates must be dashed upon the rocks, or die in a sea monster's gullet? How is that fair? You're cruel storyteller, Zahra!"

"Dunya...what are you really angry about?"

"You! You intervened with the Sultan for me, when I was due to marry him. Why did you not come sooner? Why did you not save Morgiana? Or Shirin? You tell stories about them, that's wonderful, but they're still dead. Why didn't you save them? Or even F—"

"Don't say her name." Zahra pressed a finger to Dunya's lips and darted her eyes towards the drowsing Sultan.

Dunya thought of the first Sultana, she with the yellow fall of hair, and was sad.

"It was not my choice," was Zahra's soft answer. "I do not have free will. That sets me apart from djinn, and from you. My choices are made for me."

Later, it would occur to Dunya that this was a very strange thing to say. But right now, all she said was, "Well, whoever made that choice could have saved ninety-eight lives, and chose not to..." Tears dripped down her face.

Zahra took Dunya's hand, and with a little tug, Dunya's head was in Zahra's lap, and the older woman was stroking her hair. "I am sorry. For what it is worth, I am sorry. And you know? I think Sinbad was sorry, too, for all of his friends that he lost."

"Maybe," said Dunya. "Do you want to continue the story?"

"It's late. I would rather rest."

Dunya said goodnight and crept out of the tent.

She stood blinking in the chilly wind, as dawn began to light the eastern horizon and stars blinked around her. It was so quiet, here, compared to the city. Yet, Al-Rayyan had begun life as land like this, graced only by the presence of a river.

Dunya huddled into her tent and tried to sleep, her head spinning with stories and the feeling of the wind on her face.

She couldn't sleep. It was strange. Her pillow felt rough against her cheek. Stray breezes whipped across her hands. She began to remember, step by step, a city she was no longer in, a city she had wandered through and not even noticed at the time.

She remembered the Palace harem. She remembered Morgiana, the touch of her hands. She remembered the color of Shirin's eyes. She remembered the smile of the Sultana with yellow hair. And she cried for a while, remembering the three of them.

Eventually her tears stilled, and the sunlight came through her tent's flaps. She thought about Upalu, sitting in a brazier in the silence of the harem.

"I thought Upalu wanted to leave," Dunya murmured to herself. She finally could feel herself growing sleepy. "But maybe she stayed because there was another wish she could grant. I wished for a friend. Maybe I'll have one."

When Sinbad's mother, Zummurud, said, "Well, those are six fine adventures and no mistake. But before you tell me of the seventh, perhaps you should listen to me tell some tales of my youth, if you have the stomach for them…"

"But, Mother," said Sinbad, "It was on my seventh and last voyage that I learned of the greatest wonder that our God has devised.

"My diplomatic mission to Ceylon was a success; on my voyage home, I sailed through a calm sea, when a storm blew in, apparently out of nowhere. The ship capsized, and the terrible water carried me to a rocky shore. I awoke to find myself on the edge of a golden city, gleaming with the images of wings and hawks.

I traveled to the palace of their king; I impressed him with my wit and the tales of my adventures…"

"God did well when He blessed you with a silver tongue," remarked Zummurud.

"Yes, He did, Mother. I stayed in the city as a guest of the king, and I was able to witness what I thought was a miracle: at the new moon, the people of this city shook off their clothes, gave a great shudder, and transformed into birds!"

"Did they?"

"Yes, and I wished to fly with them to see the world from on high. I did not think further ahead than my next thrilling sight. The king himself carried me up, up, up, until I was looking down from a heavenly vantage point! Such a delight! I praised God out loud—and before I knew it, the king let me go, and the people in flight set upon me, breaking my fall again and again with blows and curses. For this was a city of devil-worshippers, who had wedded themselves to demons for six generations. They would not stand to hear the name of God.

"I landed badly, and I tried to give thanks that I was alive. But it is hard to give thanks with a raucous, distant laughter in your ears. Yet I was blessed, for a good woman named Lina found me. She took pity on me and took me to her father's house, where she tended to me and told me her story. She and her father had come to the city as refugees, fleeing war. They had arrived and stayed, with nowhere else to go. They had resisted worshipping devils along with the rest of the city and accrued some small wealth as merchants.

"I hope you will not think me improper, Mother, when I said that they could come home with me, to Baghdad."

"Not improper in the least, my boy."

"It was a harder task than I had thought to leave the city, for when he resumed his human form, the king was all smiles and apologies, acting as though he had been my friend the entire time. The people wanted me to stay, wanted, I think, for me to join their ranks and disown my religion. I might have stayed—I was so weary of voyaging, and still weak from my fall—had Lina not been by my side. She and her father had resisted their false friendship and empty promises for so many years. And Lina was determined to see Baghdad. She sold the items of their household, and we purchased a small boat, and by what I knew of sailing, I managed to take us to the nearest port city of good, God-fearing humans. And from there we voyaged to Baghdad. And, Mother, may I speak freely?"

"Do you not always, my son?"

"I learned to admire Lina for her tenacity and her prudence. I learned to love her for her goodness. I have beheld the greatest wonder that God has made, and it is love. I wish for Lina to be my wife, but I would like you to meet her, first."

"I should very much like to meet this young woman. Where is she?"

"She is waiting in the other room, waiting for your permission, with all the patience that her nature permits."

The Mermaids' Parlay

The royal party returned to the city after a successful hunt. Over the next several months, every dayheld a new preparation for the coming of the heir. Dunya got used to the presence of doctors and attendants in the royal chambers. She would go into the city, often accompanied by Upalu, to get away from the little crowd.

Zahra had successfully asked for Dunya to retain her own little room. In there, by candlelight, she composed her weekly letters to Munir, which she composed faithfully and sent off, and there she also treasured his irregular but lengthy replies.

When it was time for Zahra's stories, she could always count on the Sultan yelling at all of the attendants to give him the space alone.

It was amazing, really, how long Zahra had held out. Dunya's sleep schedule had adjusted to the rhythm of falling asleep in wee hours of the morning and waking in the early afternoon. She couldn't imagine how Zahra maintained this.

Then came the night of the full moon. As usual, the Sultan began his tirade when evening turned into night:

"Every one of you, out of my sight! You've bothered me long enough, now you'll bother my best one, my queen, my entertainer? Out! Out! Nothing you have is so important it can't wait."

Dunya settled in her corner, knowing she didn't count as one of the crowd. She was invisible, an empty presence. And she quashed a sting of annoyance at what a—what was the word—what a petty tormenter the Sultan was.

Perhaps Zahra was also annoyed tonight. As soon as the attendants had left, she coaxed the Sultan out of his ill mood.

"You shouldn't take out your temper on them, sire," she said. "They mean well. They only want the best for us and the child." She put the Sultan's hand on her stomach. "Meet good intentions with goodwill."

The Sultan grumbled something in response, something Dunya didn't hear.

"You're tired. Rest a bit before I tell you tonight's story. It will be all you dreamed of and more." She began to sing, then, a soothing melody that made Dunya's eyelids flutter shut. The Sultan stretched himself out on his bed and said, "Wife, since when have you been a singer..." He was asleep before he finished the sentence.

Dunya nearly nodded off, but pinched her cheek to stay awake. "Zahra, you have a lovely voice..." she said, and when she opened her eyes, Zahra was gone.

"Oh…" Dunya grew awake again very fast. The Sultan was stretched out and fast asleep on his bed. Dunya investigated every corner of the room. "Zahra?" she whispered. "Zahra? This isn't funny."

She pulled on her blue headscarf and hurried throughout the Palace, to the library, the gardens, even the harem—anywhere she thought Zahra might have gone.

She returned to the Palace bedroom and sat at the window, hoping to catch a glimpse of Zahra somewhere on the grounds. She began to feel afraid again.

She awoke to the sound of footfalls. Zahra re-entered the bedchamber.

"Where were you?" Dunya demanded, sitting up.

"Do not be afraid," said Zahra, without looking at her. She hurried to the brazier and began to draw off her veils. A soft cry filled the room. Dunya drew closer and saw a baby in Zahra's arms. He was a sad little thing, stained in blue, but he took on a ruddier color by the fire, and began to squirm and cry.

"What have you done?" Dunya asked.

"I have given the Sultan a son," Zahra replied.

"I do not think that is the usual way that Sultans acquire sons," Dunya said, now very confused.

"Nor is this the usual fate for a stillborn child of the steppes," Zahra replied, "Yet here we are."

Dunya did not ask any more questions.

Nor was she entirely surprised when, in the morning, every attendant seemed to remember having been present for a straightforward birth that produced a healthy little boy.

The Sultan, of course, was prouder than a peacock. He named his son after his own father, Almas. Obligingly, the baby thrived. And with the succession to the throne secured, the Kingdom breathed a collective sigh of relief.

One day, ten days after the birth, Dunya had the dream again--someone trapped in the river under the Palace, crying and crying. She was supposed to take Upalu out today and had an idea.

Dunya met with Upalu in the empty harem. The djinni was in her now-comfortable human form, contemplating the disorganized chess pieces on the rug before her. Dunya had long ago forbidden Upalu from tasting the lacquered wood with fire—"Just a bit of fire, Dunya! Oh, all right"—and Upalu had no patience for the game itself.

"Come on," Dunya said, "We're going to the river today."

"The river? You keep me waiting for hours to tell me we're going to the river?" Upalu rolled her eyes and groaned, but Dunya was already heading towards the servant's door, tucking her headscarf around her chin.

"Today will be a special day. We're going to go to the First Gate, where the river meets the walls of Al-Rayyan. I have an inspiration."

"Since when do you follow inspiration?"

"Since when are you so cynical?"

"Oh, only for the past five or so centuries. Before that I was as pure as a lily and as silly as a bird."

Dunya laughed and led the way to the servant's gate. By now she knew the lay of Al-Rayyan quite well, and she led the way north, to the First Gate, with confidence.

"So what was your inspiration, exactly?" asked Upalu as they crossed over a small canal. "A dream? A vision? Did tea leaves tell you?"

"A dream," said Dunya. "I've had it before. I've dreamed of someone in water, crying out for help."

"You can't help a drowning person."

"They weren't drowning. I think they were a water spirit…"

"Even worse. Water spirits are the most fickle creatures under the sun."

"I've had this dream before, Upalu. Whatever was crying has been miserable for the better part of a year."

Upalu was silent after that, until they came into sight of the river, when she said, "Is the fishing good in this river? Because otherwise, the spears are an odd touch…"

The men and women working the river were not, strictly speaking, carrying spears, but they had tied knives to the ends of long poles and were slashing at the water as they worked. One woman, who was patrolling the water while her family unloaded bolts of cloth behind her, sank her makeshift weapon into the water only to have it torn away from her. She nearly fell in.

"Are you all right?" Dunya asked the woman when she recovered.

"Just as well as before, thank you, but that was my best knife." The woman shook a fist at the water.

"What were you knifing at the water for?" Dunya asked.

The woman looked at Dunya as though she was witless. "Where have you been? It's the damn trash-eater marids come in to the river. They'll choke Al-Rayyan dry, just you wait."

At that, the woman's husband called for a hand with a bolt, and the woman turned away. Dunya looked up at Upalu.

"Marids?" she asked.

"If there are marids in the water, I'll be damned," said Upalu. She pinched Dunya's clothes and pulled her away from the rush of traffic. "Marids prefer the ocean. They're distant cousins of mine, if you want to know the truth."

"Is that so?"

"Oh, yes. They're also in the wish-granting business. But I've never known one to come this far inland on freshwater."

"So the woman must have been mistaken."

"Certainly. If there's anything in the water, it's likely mermaids."

"Mermaids?"

"Oh, sure. Can't you smell them?"

Dunya took a good sniff and shook her head. "No, I don't smell anything other than the usual river smells."

"Yep, a nice whiff of garbage. That's mermaid smell."

Dunya wiped at her nose and asked, "And how do you know?"

"I've been out west, I've met quite a few mermaids. There's all kinds, kinds that prefer the sea, kinds that prefer the land, but none of them like to be sliced at while swimming, I know that much."

She looked at the water, where sailors were still stabbing at the water. In the press of boats, it was almost impossible to see a whole arm span of empty water, let alone anything swimming in it. She turned back to Upalu. "They aren't like wild animals, are they? They're spirits."

"That's right. They're as smart as humans." "Then why are the people attacking them?"

"Because they're damned nuisances," growled a sailor behind them. "Now will you stop trading in two-bit gossip and get out of my way?"

Dunya got out of the way, with Upalu pushing her gently until they were well out of the path of traffic.

"The nerve of him," muttered Upalu. "Some people have no manners."

"I think this is what my dream was about," said Dunya. "These mermaids are being treated unjustly."

"They don't belong in Al-Rayyan. They've never been here before."

"Then why are they here? Maybe they're just passing through. Surely they deserve to…you know…swim around without knives coming at them. Where do you think we could talk to some?"

"I think we should follow your original idea."

Dunya grinned, then pointed north. "To the First Gate!"

And so, Dunya met her first mermaid. And for a while there, she honestly wished she had not.

Upalu had not been kidding about the smell. And, as the djinni helpfully added, fire spirits didn't normally care about smell. Apparently, neither did water spirits. These freshwater mermaids smelled like garbage and all manner of waste, since that was, apparently, all that they ate.

Merfolk were also the yellowish color of unripe olives, pale on their stomachs and dapple-spotted on their backs. And at least one of them—that is, the male that was sunning himself on a bank by the First Gate—had long, handsome whiskers.

"What do you want?" he asked. He was occupying an inlet normally used as a neighborhood laundry pool. There were people going about their business, or lingering in windows and doorways. All were glancing at the insouciant merman. All mistrustful.

"I want…" Dunya tried to summon up Shirin's haughtiness, but decided that it would be better to emulate Morgiana."I want to talk to you," she said as kindly as she could manage. "Or to your leader. Chieftain? Your Sultan?"

"And why would you want to do that? To throw blades at them all?" asked the merman, stretching his arms out. He had no legs, just a long middle that tapered into a fish's tail. When he splashed it, another terrible whiff of garbage floated through the air. Dunya delicately held her headscarf over her nose.

Time to act the royal. "I am a Princess of Al-Rayyan," she said. "I would like to speak to your leader and understand your needs, if you are to live here in this city." The merman barked a laugh at that. "Well, if you insist. I'll call them up. You don't scare me by the way, fire-brat," he added, looking at Upalu before he dove under the water.

Dunya glanced up at the djinni. She looked miffed. Dunya said, "I think that went well." "Fire-brat," Upalu muttered.

"Oh, get over it."

"Dreams. We're here on account of dreams."

"Well, now we're here on account of diplomacy."

"And what gives you authority to be a diplomat?"

Dunya thought, then smiled up at her friend-sometimesenemy. "The Sultan said I could run his affairs myself. He then called me a presumptuous worm, but it's the wording, not the thought, that counts."

The merman surfaced again. "Follow me. Er...walk, if you absolutely must," he added, with something like a sneer. He then swam upriver, out the First Gate. To follow him, Dunya and Upalu had to pass through the gate for humans and look for him on the other side. Dunya had been expecting open air and wide empty plains, not a small tent city pressed right up to the wall itself.

When she expressed this thought to Upalu, the djinni said, "Well, cities grow. When taxes are high, people will live outside the city walls and do business there. This is like another bud on the tree of Al-Rayyan." She then made a face. "Ugh. I was being poetic there. Ignore that."

Dunya laughed and pulled the djinni towards the river. Out here, the river was surrounded by a recently erected fence of crude wood spikes. There were openings for wharfs and jetties, because the river was crowded with boats, if anything, more crowded than the river within the city.

"Are they also avoiding taxes?" Dunya asked, while squinting at the water to try and spot more merfolk.

"Yes, most likely."

"Taxes must be a terrible thing."

"I wouldn't know; I've never paid them."

Dunya spotted the merman at last. He was laughing at them from the center of the river.

"There he is, Upalu, he's laughing at us."

"Well, we can't have that."

"Upalu, could you grant a wish for me?"

Upalu narrowed her eyes. "What are you thinking of now?"

"To let me go to the merfolk and talk to them. Just to hear them out. Hear their story."

"You're the strangest human I've ever met."

"Is that a yes or a no?"

"You won't want to get that scarf of yours wet. Hold on."

Dunya removed her headscarf herself and handed it to Upalu. "Take good care of it. It's not mine."

"Yes, yes, I know. Now, you're sure you want to go into the river?"

"Yes."

Upalu dug her hand into a pocket and drew out a line of mud-colored cloth. She deftly tied it around Dunya's head and said, "Don't lose this. It will let you breathe and talk underwater."

"But I can't swim."

"If you wash up, I'll find you. I told you, I can only grant wishes within my own power."

"And how will you send me into the water?"

Upalu grinned. "Remember, you asked." Before Dunya could answer, Upalu picked her up, swung back, and tossed her into the river, into a gap between boats.

Whatever indignant names Dunya was going to fling at the djinni were swallowed up in an angry gurgle.

"You were serious?" asked a voice next to her. Dunya turned and saw the merman. He was head and shoulders out of the water while she was foundering. She managed a nod, and felt him take her hand, and draw her down, down, down—it was with a horrified gasp that she realized she could indeed still breathe. She couldn't smell, though, and that was a relief. Nor, she realized, could she see. Underwater was blurry and full of grit, and getting darker by the minute. She closed her eyes just to protect them and felt her guide bring her to a stop.

"You wanted to meet them, and here they are," said her guide. "Lucky for you they were in a meeting."

Dunya focused on breathing, the strange sensation of drawing in air while there was water all around her. Allah bless Upalu and her wishes.

"Who are you?" came the first watery voice. Dunya had the impression of an old woman, a matriarch that immediately reminded her of her own grandmother.

"I am Dunya, Princess of Al-Rayyan." She elected not to go into semantics just now.

"What is Al-Rayyan?" asked another voice. This one seemed younger.

No one answered, and Dunya cleared her throat, trying to get used to the clash of bubbles in her mouth and air in her lungs. "Al-Rayyan is the city that you are in now. Er, entering. Er, trying to enter…"

"Al-Rayyan is the city. But what is Al-Rayyan itself?"

"It means the watering place." Dunya giggled and gestured around her. "You know what water is, right?"

"Don't patronize us, girl!" snapped the elder. "We asked what is Al-Rayyan itself; why is the city here? What does the city mean?"

"Well…there was a story that my grandmother once told me…" Dunya's fingers covered her mouth a moment, as she remembered. Then she drew her hands away and said, "The people and the river made a deal. The river would flow through, and it would bring water. The people would live on either side, and they would give music and stories to the water, and share the water. That is how Al-Rayyan came to be."

"A pretty story. And who was your mother?"

The change in conversation confused her, but it would not do to show hesitation in front of them. "Her name was
Rashida and she had an olive grove."

"What are olives?" asked the younger voice.

"A sort of seaweed of the land," answered the elder. "Very well. Your mother was a tender of plants. That's good. You have our attention. You come before us as—what? An ambassador of the humans?"

"Yes. Why have you come to Al-Rayyan? Why now? We've never before had mermaids in our river."

"We're migrating," said another voice. This one sounded older and male. "And we're not returning." "We might not return…" said the younger voice.

"Not in my lifetime," said the older female.

"Please," said Dunya, "Could you tell me your names? It is hard to keep track…"

"Why don't we emerge," offered one, "and allow our guest a little fresh air and sunlight?"

"I hate fresh air and sunlight…"

"No one asked you, Flicker."

"Flicker" was an odd name for anyone, Dunya thought, until she felt herself moving upwards, and her head broke the surface of the water. Her guide pushed her towards a rock, where she clambered and sat, dripping endlessly. When she looked around, the light was blinding, and in the water, the light flickered.

"What are your names?" Dunya asked, blinking and trying to get a good look at her conversants. They were all merfolk—she could tell that just from the smell—and her eyes adjusted to three—no, four, counting her guide— yellowish-grayish-green forms all staring at her. All of them had handsome whiskers and no hair to speak of, and she could only guess at their ages. Clockwise from her left, they spoke:

"I am Waterfall-Climber," said the one whose voice reminded Dunya of her grandmother.

"I'm Flicker," said the one who had asked what AlRayyan was.

"Winterborn," said the other male, who had said little up to now.

"And I'm your guide," said the one directly to Dunya's right, "Strength."

"Those…those are all good names," Dunya said awkwardly. "Now…why are you leaving and not coming back?"

"All we want is to pass through this city in peace," said Winterborn, "because our home lake has become poisoned. It is no longer safe to live there, so we decided to try our luck moving downriver."

"We might not find a safe habitat," said Flicker mournfully.

"We are the bottom-feeder merfolk," said WaterfallClimber, sternly, "We will always find a place to live. Don't mind her," she said to Dunya, "She was born at the dark of the moon; she can't help it."

"The lake is poisoned?" Dunya asked. "How? By what? The poison will eventually come here, to the city."

Winterborn shook his head. "Do not worry about it. It originated here."

Dunya bit her tongue on an exclamation and said, "I would appreciate it if you explained that, please."

"What good manners!" said Waterfall-Climber. "Whoever raised you, raised you right."

"Thank you. Why do you say the poison originated here? Is Al-Rayyan already sickened?" Dunya thought about the city she had walked in just this morning. The markets were as busy as ever, the soldiers still drilling in the northeastern quadrant, the storytellers loud and melodic in the cafés. How could it be sickening? Dying? Tears sprang into her eyes at the thought.

"Oh, but we can't expect you to feel it. You're just a human," said Flicker, splashing her tail anxiously. The shadows of the wooden fence seemed to fall heavily on her.

"Are you saying-" Dunya lowered her voice, because the subject was almost too horrible to even contemplate, let alone vocalize, "Are you saying there is a plague here?"

"Oh, no, nothing as literal as that," said Flicker. "But the center of Al-Rayyan—the person that everyone should follow —don't you understand? Your moon and sun. Your—what is the word?"

"Your chieftain," said Waterfall-Climber. "The first human of this city."

"The Sultan?" Dunya pushed a strand of hair out of her eyes. "You're saying his illness is what's infecting the city?"

"And it infected our home. We fall within the borders, as you humans have drawn them up." Waterfall-Climber gave a sniff and traced her whiskers with one finned hand. "And the chieftain here has been acting wrongly, so deeply wrongly that it is poisoning us."

Dunya leaned forward and covered her eyes. The water seemed suddenly far too bright for all of this. "I know this. I know that he is ill. But I don't understand how what one man does—even a Sultan—can affect you, far away, or why it means that you have to come here."

"The Mandate of Heaven," said Winterborn, to an impressive silence.

"What he means by that," said Waterfall-Climber, "is if the ruler does not act in accordance with what God wills, then the water and people will suffer. Well, you would say the land would suffer." She gave a little scoff.

"How did your water suffer, though?" Dunya asked.

"We are weakening," said Strength, abruptly. He had not spoken much throughout this exchange. "Our seers' mirrors and knots no longer have potency. For the past year, our life has been in crisis, but we hoped it would get better, and instead…we are trying another water."

"Wait…you said it's been a year?" Dunya asked. The answer came in the affirmative, from all four.

She thought quickly. A year ago…well, nine months ago had been the hunting trip, and a month before that, Dunya had married the Sultan, and three months before that had been the death of his first wife, and then he had begun executing the women of the harem.

"A year and a month ago was when the Sultan first went mad." She paused, then said, "I should have known. Upalu warned me. I should have worked harder to find a remedy. But nine months passed and I forgot, and…"

"You are just one girl," said Waterfall-Climber, in what she probably meant to be a kindly voice "and not even fully grown at that."

I am fully grown, Dunya thought, miffed.

"You say you are a Princess, and you have the smell about you."

"You can tell?" Dunya asked. She couldn't help herself; her own nose had shut down some five minutes ago.

"You have the smell of important waters about you. It's a matter of where you live. I don't expect you to know. All we ask is that you speak to the others of importance, and let us pass through the river here without injury. Some of us are attempting the passage. Most return, bearing stab wounds and slices for their trouble."

"I'm so sorry to hear that."

"Fortunately, God has made us tough."

"Don't attempt the crossing again," Dunya said to them. "If you would take my advice, wait, and…and I will speak to the Viziers on your behalf. I will come up with a way for you to pass in safety. I am sorry that you have to leave your home."

"We may return," said Flicker.

"Not in my lifetime," grumbled Winterborn.

"Thank you," said Waterfall-Climber. "Strength will escort you back to where you were…how did you enter the river? Jumped?"

"I was thrown," Dunya said, with a small glare towards wherever Upalu was.

"Very well, Strength will throw you out again. Strength?"

"No! No—I'll just walk back."

"Really? Those legs seem so precarious…not like a good, reliable tail."

"I'll manage somehow. Thank you. I will return here at… this time, say…"

"Tomorrow."

"I was hoping for more time…"

"So were we, but we must make our passage soon. We cannot crowd this part of the river much longer."

"Understood. I will be here at this time tomorrow."

"Then we can ask for no more."

The four merfolk disappeared beneath the surface of the water, Strength remaining a moment longer to nod a farewell to Dunya. She got to her feet unsteadily and saw Upalu waiting on the other side of the fence of stakes.

"I told you I'd find you," the djinni said to Dunya.

Dunya peeled off the sodden headband while Upalu pulled up the stakes with ease. "This was handy, but not as useful as I'd hoped."

"Oh, well. Whatever is?" said Upalu, as she pulled out two more stakes and made an opening just wide enough for Dunya to slip through. Now Dunya thoroughly stank of the river, and they made their way back to the Palace.

"I ignored the Sultan's illness," said Dunya to the djinni. "But now I must redouble my search for a remedy. I hadn't realized that his illness would affect the length and breadth of the Kingdom. I must research this and find a cure for him, as soon as I have found a way for the merfolk to pass through in peace…"

"One thing at a time," Upalu advised her. "Why don't you start by telling me what those catfish told you?"

It took the rest of the walk to the Palace to explain. After a bath to wash the smell of fish off of her and dispel the river's chill, Dunya dressed herself again, but not as a street-ready servant girl. She had requested a few outfits from the Palace tailors and dressmakers, outfits fit for more formal occasions. She donned one such outfit now and went in search of her father.

He was easy to find; in his office as usual, even though the sun was setting.

"Hello," she said, standing in the door of his office. "I wish to speak with you."

"It's you," he said, without much feeling either of joy or of sadness. "What do you want from me?"

"I want to talk to you about the river trade. It's important…" she hesitated between the two titles she knew for him and said, "Vizier Shareef."

At that, he looked up at her and seemed hurt. "And what do you know of the river trade?"

"I know that there are mermaids swimming through the river, trying to pass, but humans are standing in their way.
What will you do to help them?"

"I have enough on my plate as it is. The mermaids should have thought about the risks before they came to this city."

"They had no choice."

"How do you know?"

"Because I spoke to them this afternoon. I made a parlay."

He started back and clutched a scroll to him with alarm. "You parlayed? On behalf of the government of Al-Rayyan?"

"Well, no one else was going to do it."

"Dunya," he began, "Princess though you may be, you are still just a child who has no idea what she's meddling with…"

"Princess I may be," she said, "and much thanks to you for that. But if I'm going to be a Princess, I may as well use what authority I have for good."

"Authority?" he barked with laughter.

"Listen to me! I—I am trying," she said. "Which is more than anyone else seems willing to do for the merfolk. Will you listen to me…Father?"

The word tasted bitter on her tongue, but he put aside the documents in his hand. "Fine. Tell me what you…" he waved a hand.

"I observed," said Dunya, patiently, "And I suggest…"

She explained her visit of earlier, and her ideas about how the situation might be resolved. He shook his head when she suggested that the merfolk might perhaps stay in Al-Rayyan.

"Never. They would disrupt our trade permanently, and without our trade, what are we?"

"We're a city—the Generous City—and shouldn't we be open to everyone?"

"Without our trade, we are a husk waiting for the wind to blow us away. No. If the merfolk want to leave, then they should—nay, must—leave."

"Then they should be able to pass through unhindered, wouldn't you agree? Unhindered by knives, by ships…"

"Ships?"

"Yes, Father."

"What did I just tell you about the trade in our city?"

"We won't die if the ships stop for just one day."

"You are only a Princess. I've had enough of your ideas for one day."

Dunya narrowed her eyes and clenched her fists, but she knew when it was no more use arguing with her father.

She turned and left quietly.

"So?" asked Upalu, when Dunya returned to her chambers. "How did it go?"

"Remember," said Dunya, "the Sultan gave me authority to meddle in the city affairs as I see fit."

"It didn't go well, did it?"

"I'm going to start meddling."

The first thing to do was to tell the people of the river to live in peace with their fishy, smelly neighbors. This, Dunya accomplished by crossing to those neighborhoods on foot, with Upalu beside her. Then Dunya would wish for an audience, and by Upalu's magic, her voice would carry far and wide to the people at work, as Dunya very firmly suggested that they set down their tools and makeshift weapons, and listen to what she had to say.

She explained that the merfolk were merely passing through, and requested a day to let them go by unharmed, no boats crashing them or knives slashing them.

The boat people protested this, but Dunya told them, "Your Sultan requests this," and they fell silent.

And Dunya assumed that it was Upalu's magic that made people not only hear her, but listen. She went first down the river, then up the river to meet with the merfolk chieftains—this time, with no undignified throwing into the water, although Upalu suggested it with a grin.

The chieftains agreed to her plan, but reluctantly. One day to pass through the city meant swimming downriver faster than they would have liked. "We are slow-going creatures, as God made us," explained Waterfall-Climber, but they agreed.

Dunya returned to the Palace, and with Upalu, she took great cuttings of the water lilies in the Palace's Lotus Garden. She wished that Upalu would restore the cut flowers, which Upalu did— to the best of her ability. And then Dunya took the flowers back to the merfolk chieftains.

"Let this be our symbol of peace," she said. "Carry these before you, and everyone will know you are under the protection of the Palace."

"But are we?" asked Waterfall-Climber. "Have you spoken to your Sultan about us?"

"No," said Dunya slowly. "He is hard to talk to. But if everyone thinks you have the protection of the Palace, then no one will dare to hurt you, and it will be nearly the same thing."

"You should have seen it," wrote Dunya to Munir, a few days later. "The river traffic stopped and the boats all moored, the city still like I've never seen it before. And then the flowers drifting on the water, and the mermaids under the flowers.

Oh, the complaints are still coming in—will still come in for another moon, or so the Vizier of Trade tells me—but the day to stop the boats has come and gone, and the people, I think, enjoyed the spectacle of the mermaids passing through.

I think you would have liked the sight of it. They cleverly knotted the water lilies that I brought into a great garland, one for the front of their procession, another for the back. I stood by the Second Gate, waiting for them to arrive and then leave the city, and it took hours for them to all pass through. But they are gone now, and I wish them well, and I do think our city would have been richer for them staying in it. But they must obey their Mandate of Heaven. I have done the best I could. I hope Morgiana would be proud of me.

Also, you need not fear, I know the Lotus Garden was a project of your mother's. I made a wish, which Upalu granted, and the water lilies are, well, they are not blooming again, but they are recovering. They will heal. So, I hope, will we all.

Your faithful servant, Dunya.

The Captain and the Djinn

Dunya would have resumed her search for a remedy for the Sultan's illness with renewed fervor the next day, but when she woke up in the early afternoon, there was a clamor in the Palace and she was surprised to find that it was about her.

It seemed that somebody had been going to one Vizier after another, trying to find who had settled the accord with the merfolk. Finally the Vizier of Trade ferreted out Dunya's hiding spot in the kitchen, where she was eating breakfast. She was still licking thyme from her fingers when the Vizier of Trade brought her to the receiving room.

"If you want to govern, learn the first lesson," he said through a clenched smile, as he led her to the room.

"What's that?" she asked, with a glare.

"Consequences," he hissed. Then his smile cleared and he said, "If you seek the heroine of yesterday's passage, this is she, the Princess Dunya."

"This one?" came the Sultan's voice. "Are you sure?"

"Yes," said the Vizier of Trade. "I am absolutely sure."

Dunya didn't say anything, but she stared down at her shoes, hearing her heartbeat in her ears.

"You. Dunya. Look up at me."

She obeyed and saw that the Sultan did not even look as if Dunya were a particularly interesting person to talk to. "I would have expected it of Zahra," he said, "She has a certain bold streak about her, for all that she acts modest. But you? Parlaying with merfolk in my city?" He leaned onto his elbows. "What gave you the idea?"

Dunya remained silent, but jumped when he yelled.

"Answer me!"

"The merfolk needed help," she said in her usual small voice, looking down. "They came to the city and people were attacking them, and I just decided I would go…meet with them…listen to them. And the idea came to me that they could just…pass through, in peace. And there need be no more bloodshed."

"What made you think you had authority to act in my name?"

Dunya took a moment to gather her courage before she answered. She looked him straight in the eye. This was no time for modesty. She thought instead of Shirin and her

Falcon-princess. "You said so, my Lord. Do you remember?"

The Sultan tilted his head. "What? When?"

"The evening after Zahra started to tell the tale of

Yasmeen. You said, 'If you are so intent on the affairs of the Kingdom, you can run them, you ignorant worm.' Those were your exact words."

She heard a sharp intake of breath from the Vizier of Trade.

"Is that so?" asked the Sultan. He leaned back.

"That is so," Dunya said. She wondered, for a moment, if she was going to die.

But instead of getting mad, the Sultan just smirked. "Huh. My temper got in the way again. Serves me right." He stood up. "You took authority from that? From a fit of temper? You're much bolder than I thought." He narrowed his eyes. "Zahra put you up to it, didn't she?" Dunya elected not to say anything.

"Well. You seized authority and used it fairly well. There was no bloodshed and now my city has more of a reputation for diplomacy. You might have thought about Al-Rayyan's reputation…it does not do to appear weak…but you did tolerably well, as my father would say. If you ever want to try something like that again, ever, you talk to me. Do you understand?"

Dimly, she understood she was not going to die. Not for this. Not yet. "I understand, sire."

"Good. Now get out; I'm tired."

A handful of mermaids did remain in the city of AlRayyan. These were the oldest, the sickest, those without a family to help them hurry down the river. These clustered around the Second Gate, gathering strength for a further voyage. Strength himself remained with them, and Dunya visited the small community every day.

"Soon we shall be off of your hands," was what Strength promised each time she came to visit. But time passed, and the mermaids remained. The healthiest among them found work, repairing boats or ferrying small packages across the river. This earned them goodwill among the people of Second Gate's neighborhoods. After one week of the merfolk living there, Dunya spotted a human housewife leaving a pot of remedies on a stone on the riverbank, and she called back from the safety of her house, that she heard someone coughing in the river every night.

"I swear, Princess, we shall be off of your hands soon," Strength said to Dunya, as she sat beside the Gate itself, in the shadowy area that the merfolk liked.

"You seem to be adapting well," Dunya said, through her headscarf (she still had not gotten used to the smell).

"Bottom feeders are excellent at adapting," Strength replied.

"Will you take that remedy?"

"Oh, of course." Strength took the small jar and held it close to him. "Droplet's got a terrible case of the wheezes. She'll be happy to have anything."

"I want to speak to you on that very subject," Dunya said. "About remedies. Do you remember what Winterborn said, about the city falling sick because the Sultan was sick?"

"Yes."

"I have been trying to find out all that I can about ways to heal, but I have no training and it is hard to get the ingredients in the Palace. They call for living animals, such as unicorns and caladrius—I don't think I've ever seen one in my life. I just wondered if you might have a remedy or two on hand—if the Sultan is cured, maybe you can return to the lake where you lived."

"Maybe," said Strength, with a guarded look in his eyes. "According to our lore, the horns of narwhals have certain healing properties…"

"What's a narwhal?"

"Point taken. Well, a wish from a marid is always…ah, but we're far from the sea, aren't we? To tell you the truth, we bottom-feeders rarely get sick. When we do get sick, we mostly leave recovery in the hands of God, blessed be His name."

"You must have something," Dunya urged.

"Well, when one of us gets sick…up here…" he tapped the side of his head, "as can happen, sometimes, with bad luck or after terrible events…we set the sick person to work tying knots."

"Knots? Out of what?"

"Grasses, weeds, anything that's handy. A lot of knots."

"That's it?"

"And they talk about how they feel."

"Oh." This struck a chord with Dunya. Hadn't she helped Upalu by just listening to her talk? "They talk, and someone else listens?"

"Well, maybe someone listens. Or we just leave them to their knot-making." He shrugged. "Healing is a lot of work. To be honest, humans put more work into healing than we do. Maybe you should ask another human?"

Dunya paused. "Thank you," she said stiffly.

"Always happy to repay a favor, Princess."

When Dunya returned to the Palace, she went straight to the great library, where she was reading through a treatise on diseases of the liver. She was surprised to find the Sultan there, deep in discussion with two Viziers. She eavesdropped for a while, but as all that they were talking about was trade and borders, she got bored and read some more about the liver. Presently she heard the Viziers leave. She risked a peek around the corner of one shelf, and saw the Sultan, alone, looking over a book of Persian illuminations.

Dunya returned the book of liver diseases to the shelf, because she smelled an opportunity in the offing. She approached the Sultan cautiously and cleared her throat.

He glanced up. "Oh, it's you," he said. "My little sisterin-law. What do you want?" He turned back to the book.

"I want to ask if you are well, your Majesty," she told him, "and to know if there is anything I can do for you."

"I am as well as ever. Slept well this morning," the Sultan remarked.

"Are you quite sure you feel well?" Dunya pressed.

The Sultan glanced up at her, annoyed now. "Why do you ask? Is there something I should know about?"

"No, nothing, sire—I'm just concerned about you. There, actually, there is something you should know about."

"Ah!" the Sultan sat up and slammed the book shut. "A plot against me. I knew it. Name the conspirators."

"It is not a plot, sire! I swear, no one is plotting against you…"

That I know of, she thought.

"It is just that…the merfolk, those who passed through the city the other day…You remember?" "How could I forget?" he asked drily.

"They told me that they were fleeing the lake that was their home because it had sickened. They said that the illness had its root in you."

"In me?"

"Yes. I don't understand it very well, but I wanted to… well, I don't like the sound of Al-Rayyan growing sick, and that is just what they spoke of. Sickness."

"But I feel healthy as a horse. Except that I never get quite enough sleep…"

"And…sire, your mind and spirit?"

"What about them?"

"Health, um, health includes spiritual and mental wellbeing…" Dunya began to shrink in on herself. What was she doing, talking medicine with this strange man that, come to the point of it, she barely knew?

Because God has put him in charge of our city, and if this Sultan sickens, then…she thought. "I wanted to make sure you were all right," she finished weakly.

The Sultan considered for a moment. Then he said, "If those mermaids had a word about my health, I rather wish I'd had the chance to talk to them before they all left. Get them to tell what they really mean. But you are genuinely concerned for me?" When Dunya nodded, he tilted his head. "Fancy that. Most everyone I know has only ever been concerned for me because of my position. They want to gain a little power for themselves. It's…lonely, to tell the truth of it," he leaned on the table with his elbow and rubbed his beard. "But here you are, concerned for me for my own sake. And no benefit to yourself?"

"No benefit to yourself," the Sultan answered his own question. "That's a first, in all my life. I will remember this kindness," he said. "I am not kind, but I can recognize it in others. Someday, I will figure out how to reward you. Now go away."

"Yes, sire."

Eventually, Dunya and the Sultan left the library and headed, side by side, towards the Sultan's bedchambers. There they would take their dinner and, of course, listen to Zahra's stories. They crossed several hallways in silence, and finally Dunya felt it was all too awkward to endure.

"Your Majesty," she asked him, "what do you like best about Zahra's stories?"

The Sultan glanced at her. "Why do you need to ask? They're wonderful."

"Yes, they are." She would not press the issue, the man was already annoyed with her. So she was surprised to hear him say, "I love how inventive the stories are. I can never tell just what will come next. I like being kept waiting."

After a time, Dunya asked, "Your Majesty, if it is not impertinent..."

"What is it?"

"What is your story, sire? If you were to sum up the story of your life...how would it sound?"

"It would be a story much like the hundreds of Sultans who came and died before me. I was born to a Sultan, and from the moment of my birth, they predicted I would have a great destiny— aren't all the Sultans gifted with great destinies? When I was four, I learned to ride a horse; when I was six, to shoot an arrow; when I was ten, I could take a hand in the appointment or dismissal of Palace officials. So, I grew into power, just as my father had, and his father before him." The Sultan stopped on the stairwell and looked at Dunya. "You're trying to figure out how I became 'ill,' aren't you?"

"Well…yes. You do not sound happy."

"I've told you before, I'm very happy. The whole city rises and falls at my bidding. And I'm not cursed with ambition, like some of our neighbors. The size of Al-Rayyan suits me nicely, so long as everyone knows their place and knows me."

Something in his tone chilled Dunya. He did not ask for her story, she noticed.

A few days later, it was the Feast of the Sacrifice, and Dunya and Upalu leaned on the Palace walls. Tonight, the cavalrymen returned to Al-Rayyan and the Palace would celebrate them. But they hadn't shown up yet—or if they had, they were still passing through the welcoming city.

"I got in a little bit of trouble with the Sultan," Dunya said.

"Nothing too bad, I hope," Upalu replied, glancing at her.

"You have something to do with it. He wanted to know why I took the issue of the mermaids in hand."

"You're soft-hearted."

Dunya didn't dispute it. "If I am, it was your magic that helped make it possible."

"So I got you in trouble, is what you're saying?"

"No." Dunya took a deep breath. "I hate being in trouble. But this was my responsibility. All you did was help."

Upalu blew out the breath she'd been holding. "I wish…" She looked at her hands. "I wish I could help more. But my magic is still…"

"Don't worry about your magic."

"I'll worry all I want! Sorry…it's just…I should be over her by now. I should be able to help you more."

"Don't worry about it. You do enough. Honestly? Having you listen to me is a help all by itself." Dunya looked over at Upalu. The djinn wore a faint smile. "I'm serious."

"I'm glad to hear that. Aha! Here they come. Now which one is your friend?"

"That one." Dunya pointed. Munir was riding in front, on a high stepping bay. He was wearing the same ceremonial robes as the first time Dunya had met him.

"He's looking for you," Upalu remarked.

"No, he's not." Dunya kept her face stoic, knowing that Upalu was watching her for a blush.

"He's looking for someone, anyway. There they go through the gates."

They watched until the last row disappeared, then Dunya said, "I had better get going."

"Be sure to smuggle me some tidbits."

"I will." They had agreed some months ago that Upalu had better keep out of the Palace eye. If the kitchen ever wondered at Dunya's capacity for food, which she requested politely and then took out of sight, they said nothing.

Dunya bid Upalu goodbye and headed towards the activity. She arrived in time to see a bit of the Sultan's welcome speech. Munir stood with his head high, his helmet tucked under one arm. Dunya couldn't catch his eye.

The feast was a similarly inane affair—many speeches and toasts made in honor of the brave and loyal border guard. Dunya had no chance to speak to Munir. She stashed what food she could in an extra scarf and snuck out as soon as the first families began to leave.

The windows of the harem were lit up. Dunya hurried in. At least thirty lamps on various surfaces were lit, without any scent of burning oil, Dunya noticed. "Upalu?" she called. "I brought you food."

Upalu stepped out from behind a screen. Her cinnamoncolored scarf was down around her shoulders, and she smiled. "That smells delicious!"

They settled down at a low table, Dunya explaining the unusual foods to Upalu and telling her about the feast. Upalu had just started on a pastry when she looked up, past Dunya, and her expression turned confrontational.

"What is it?" Dunya turned and saw Munir, in the doorway of the harem.

"Hello," he said, uncertainly. "What are you...? Never mind. I'll leave."

"No, no, come in, Captain!" Dunya got to her feet. In the corner of her eye, Upalu tugged her scarf over her hair.

"What are you doing here?" Upalu asked, none too friendly.

"I was...look, Morgiana was..." Munir clenched his teeth, looking for the right words.

"You make a habit of walking in on women?" "Upalu," Dunya said warningly.

"Morgiana was my friend,and I miss her. I wondered if I could find anything of her in the harem. I thought it was empty."

"You won't tell," Dunya said, with urgency. "No one knows she lives here."

"Who is she?"

"She's Upalu. She's my friend."

Munir looked between the two of them, considering, and then said, "If she's your friend, that's good enough for me." "Won't you join us?" Dunya asked.

"He'll be missed at his own feast," Upalu remarked. When Dunya glared at her, Upalu said, "I'm just saying."

"I made my excuses...I was sufficiently well-mannered. Don't worry on my account."

Dunya somehow doubted that Upalu was worried. She took a deep breath and thought, How would Morgiana approach this? The answer came clear: with grace and care.

"Upalu," she said, "This is my friend Munir. I've told you about him. Munir, meet my friend Upalu. Now you can be friends, yourselves."

Munir settled himself at the table and took a pastry, just to be polite. He looked around. "Who lit the lamps?" "I did," Upalu said.

"It makes a beautiful effect."

"Thank you."

"How did you...come to live in the Palace?"

"I'm her lady-in-waiting." Upalu jerked her head towards Dunya.

"Oh. And what is your family?"

"The Ember family."

Munir blinked. "I don't know them."

"Munir," Dunya said, "I brokered a treaty with mermaids...and Upalu is..."

"Ah ah ah," Upalu said. She held up a warning finger.

Dunya fell silent.

"A mermaid?" Munir finished, looking between them.

"Do you see a tail?" Upalu snorted. "You should have brought more food, Dunya."

"I'll bring a sack next time," Dunya said drily. "Anyway— Upalu helped me with the mermaids." Upalu nodded.

"Then I am in the presence of two diplomats. I admire your work," Munir said. "If I had a glass, I would toast to you."

"But we don't have anything to drink. Dunya." Upalu glared at her.

"I can't carry everything!" When Upalu snickered, Dunya slumped. "Don't tease me like that."

"If you had known we were having company..."

"I can leave...I can take a hint," Munir said, starting to stand up.

"That wasn't a hint directed at you, don't give yourself too much credit," Upalu said.

"Upalu, manners!" Dunya said.

"What's wrong with my manners?"

"This is the most honest conversation I've had in the Palace since…in a very long time," Munir said. "I quite enjoy the candor. And I won't give myself too much credit in future."

"How should we credit you? What is your rank?" Upalu asked.

"Captain. Captain of the Border Patrol."

"Probably passed down from your old man."

"Upalu!" Dunya said. "I'm sure he earned it on his own."

"No, it's partially true. My father led the Palace guard. I chose the borders, when I came of age."

Now Dunya was curious. "Why did you?" she asked.

Munir picked up an empty cup and tossed it between his hands. "I like the borders…you can hear yourself think out there. The sky is wide open…"

"And it's safer than the Palace," Upalu suggested.

Munir glanced at her. He gave a half nod, but said nothing.

"Don't put words in his mouth," Dunya said to Upalu. To Munir she asked, "Why did you?"

He spoke slowly. "I'm not really a warrior by any stretch. I'm quite cowardly by nature."

"No, you're not," Dunya said.

Munir almost smiled. "I'm touched by your faith in me. I try to stay out of…well, what you might call the saga of our Kingdom. I'm happy to have a little role. Barely a verse, and back to the main thread—that's me."

"But what's your story?" Dunya urged. "Yours? Munir's?"

"I…don't know. I'm a man who likes to tool leather, in my spare time. I gifted Morgiana a lamp, once. It was copper. She laughed, because the harem…" He gestured around himself, "already has an abundance of lamps. That's something, I guess."

"If I have any courage, I've learned it by visiting AlRayyan, disguising my station and walking along the river like any other girl and learning its stories. Munir, would you join me? There's freedom in it."

He laughed at the absurdity of it, then saw that she was serious. "If you wish me, I will gladly accompany you," he said.

"Tomorrow, then."

"As you wish, my lady."

"Speaking of stories…" Upalu raised her eyebrows at Dunya.

"Oh!" Dunya got to her feet. "Thank you for reminding me. —I apologize for the abrupt exit, but Zahra's stories! I have to be there. Thank you—both of you—goodbye!" And she hurried out of the harem.

"Now, son," said Sinbad's mother Zummurud, "You have said your tales, and it is time for me to tell mine, if you will listen…

"Before he married me, your father built a house, and I glowed with happiness when I came there as a new bride. But the house was cursed, and we could not understand how. The garden plants died, even though the well water was clear and cold; the walls cracked over the years; servants would fall ill, and it took me many years to conceive a child. I had almost given up hope when you came along, and I wept when your horoscope was read. You were born under a wandering star, so I knew that the day would come when you would leave me.

"There came a plague to our house, in the first year of your life. The houses to either side of us were untouched, but our house—ah! But of course, we sickened. Our servants' children lay in fevers on cots. Our well, horrors!
Our well went dry.

"My lord husband went to seek the best doctor in the city. But I had— call it woman's intuition—I had a feeling that the root of our troubles went far, far deeper. I heard a voice from the bottom of the well, and scritches and scratches. When my husband went for the doctor, I left the housekeeper in charge of the sickbeds, tied you to my back, and ventured down into the well, carrying a torch.

"Under the well, there lurked a miserable ghost of a man. His house had stood on our property, in ages past. When alive, he had invited greed into his heart, and now his soul remained trapped, bound to this world.

"I brandished my torch in his face and told him he damn well ought to leave this property and move on or else he'd regret it. I never was one for diplomacy.

"In response, he made my torch go out.

"I thought—still think—that was playing dirty. I was terrified. But I held on tight to the charred stick and found a wall, and I wrote the name of God in the wall, with the charcoal. After that, the ghost couldn't touch me. I summoned up a little pity for him and prayed to God for his soul. And God, the Merciful, the bringer of light into darkness, heard my prayer and the ghost vanished. The well filled with water quickly enough, but I always had a knack for swimming and I climbed out of the well with you no worse for the wear. My husband was shocked to hear of my exploits, but he was glad to know he was married to a successful exorcist. Our servants recovered, our house stood strong, and our garden thrived. And it was after that, my dear little voyager, that your brother the homebody was born.

"That is one way that a woman may protect her home."

Waking Up

When Dunya met Munir outside the Palace kitchens the next day, she had to stop herself from laughing out loud with delight. Munir wore no sashes or ornaments befitting a Captain, but just the raiment of a low-ranking cavalryman from his own unit—his uniform in daily life.

"You look perfect," Dunya told him. "Come on, let's go."

They took Dunya's favorite walking route over the First Bridge, into the theater district. There, they ate falafels from a street vendor and walked through a public park built by a royal grant. Dunya showed Munir her favorite mosque, and he admired the calligraphy of the tiles around the door, and gave generously to all of the beggars waiting there. Dunya attempted to tell him one of Zahra's stories, but she forgot incidents and misnamed characters and bungled it up until her cheeks burned, but Munir told her he liked it all the same. Then he began to tell one of his stories, about his early days on the borders, and how he had to befriend and master the most skittish horse in the cavalry. That was shortly after his father died—he abruptly stopped when he mentioned his father.

"Are you all right?" Dunya asked him.

"I'm well. Just reminded of parts of the past I would rather forget."

"I'm sorry," Dunya said. "Fathers can be…difficult."

"Mine was not difficult, so much, as he was very distant," said Munir. "He was more focused on the Sultan's upbringing than on mine." He paused.

"That sounds lonely. For you," Dunya offered.

"It was a demanding job. For many people." He frowned and looked off at the river.

"What's the matter?"

"My cousin…" Munir began. He checked over his shoulder, and then behind Dunya. "There was…an accident, when he was a boy. Sword training. The—my cousin was always deft with weapons. I wasn't sure how this accident had happened, unless…"

"Unless it wasn't," Dunya said in a low voice. "Was it?"

"I don't ask," Munir said, and his voice was almost a whisper. "My cousin was disciplined soundly and he performed all the rites and payments that are fitting and proper. I don't ask any more of him. I ask nothing more of him, as much as I can help it."

An image flashed into Dunya's head: Munir, standing with his helmet under his arm, in front of the Sultan, telling of the safety and security of Al-Rayyan.

"That's why you're on the borders," Dunya said. "Not particularly that I belong there," Munir said, "But I didn't belong in this city either. You already know Al-Rayyan better than I ever did." He straightened up from the railing and stretched his back. "The fresh air does me good. My domain is hills and high plains, and my men are loyal, even on a fool's mission. And if I lived here more, I might be a danger to you."

"A danger to me?" Dunya asked. "What are you talking about?"

Munir smiled again, and this time there was certainly something rueful in his expression. "I'll explain another time. How about we get back to the Palace?"

That night, Dunya dreamed of the water again.

She dreamed only briefly of the river, drenched in the early morning sunlight, and Munir, reaching for her hand but not looking in her eyes. Then her dream turned to the Palace, the lake below the Palace, and once again, she heard that wretched sobbing in the darkness.

She wanted to go down and see who was crying. "I want to go down," she said out loud, and her dream obeyed her. She descended through the water and could see, though there was no light. She saw a woman, bent with grief, on the bottom of the cistern, with strange jewelry—bangles and bracelets of a far Northern style—littering the water around her. The woman began to cry, and then to scream, and her piercing shriek woke Dunya up with a start.

She gasped, bewildered to find herself in dry air instead of deep underwater. She clambered out of bed, dressed hurriedly, and ran to find Zahra. She was easy to find this morning, in her own chamber, entertaining the baby Prince. Two Palace nursemaids were answering her questions about the baby's welfare. Dunya interrupted all this.

"Zahra," said Dunya, "Zahra?"

"I'm busy right now," said Zahra, barely sparing a glance from the baby.

"I need to talk to someone." She felt peevish and still agitated from her dream.

"This Palace is full of people. You don't need to talk to me, do you? If you do, then all you need to do is wait."

Dunya seethed. She went and got dressed with her blue headscarf, and ate a hurried breakfast, but she did not return to the Sultan's chambers. She stalked the Lotus Garden for a while, but Munir did not appear. She went to the harem, but Upalu still slept in her brazier. Cursing the infidelity of men and djinn, Dunya wound her way to the kitchen, grabbed a pita full of lamb for lunch, and went into the city.

She walked along the streets going directly for the neighborhoods she usually avoided. She eyed ruffians and unsavory-looking characters, who let her go by without so much as a glance. She felt secure in the power of the blue headscarf, but thinking of that only reminded her of the older woman, and every time that she had hid, or deflected, or condescended, or merely smiled instead of giving a proper answer. So Dunya wrenched her thoughts from these musings, and tried to focus on what was around her. But it did not go very well.

She stopped at a small well to eat her lamb pita and have a sip of water. The well was situated in a square, where old women chattered in the shade and old men played at checkers. Dunya spotted another girl, about her own age, coming to draw water for her family.

"Peace upon you," Dunya said to her.

"And upon you," replied the girl. She leaned on her pitcher, evidently glad for a little conversation. "I haven't seen you in this neighborhood before."

"I'm passing through. I have a question."

"You think I may have an answer?"

"Well, maybe. This may be an answer found before a spinning wheel, not in a book."

"I like the sound of that."

"If one wanted to contact the spirit of the river, the spirit that was here before Al-Rayyan was founded, where would one have to go?"

The girl's smile vanished. "You would have to be very desperate to do that. I heard a story that, before I was born, my grandfather's younger brother wanted to talk to the river. He failed, and it claimed his life."

"But how did he go about it?"

"He worked in the Palace…"

"I work in the Palace," Dunya offered.

"It must have been some way in there. Our Lord knows, the river in the daylight would never hear you over all the boats and shouting."

"Then you mean it was the cistern? There's a lake underneath the Palace…"

Now the girl looked frightened. "I wouldn't go to the Palace if you paid my dowry in gold and diamonds."

"Why not?" Dunya asked.

"What, do you mean you don't know? You work there, don't you?"

Dunya's mind worked terribly fast. "Do you mean the Sultan?"

As soon as she said that, the clattering of game pieces ceased, and the old women's voices stopped. Dunya was aware of every eye in the square resting on her, and of a horror that chilled the stifling air.

"You work in the Palace," murmured the girl that she had been talking to. She hastily pulled up her ewer and said, "Allowances must be made." Then she left without a formal goodbye.

Dunya, still thirsty, stared after her bewildered. Then she ate her lamb pita and left almost as quickly, still feeling the stares of the neighborhood behind her.

While she had been walking by herself, she had never yet crossed a bridge. She had wandered quite far south by this time, and she decided she would cross to the eastern portion of the city to see what she could see there. But, unbeknownst to Dunya, she crossed by the headquarters of the Beggar's Guild. She was walking down the street, observing that this street had much more litter and piles of old clothes than other streets had. Then, suddenly, one of the piles of old clothes—or what she had mistaken for a pile of old clothes—sat up and asked her for money.

Dunya leapt back and shrieked with shock; other beggars appeared, and all they did was ask for pennies, but Dunya felt besieged on all sides. She ran for it—ran for the one building that she knew would have an open door for her: a small, whitewashed mosque.

She caught her breath once she was in the cool shade. She heard voices and the shuffling of bodies in the space beyond. She had almost forgotten what time it was.

"I shall stay for afternoon prayer," she whispered to herself.

It had been a long and strange day already. Although the setting was foreign, it was soothing to go through the rituals of washing and preparation. She sat on the woman's side of the congregation; there were a few other women present, all mothers or grandmothers of the neighborhood. She faced Mecca, bowed, and prayed, paying attention to the imam's words, and uttering her responses in a soft voice.

Goodness. When had been the last time she had meaningfully prayed, paying attention and everything? She thought with a wince of how often she had knelt and bowed, but her mind had been occupied with Zahra's wonderful stories. She put away her own shame and bowed, thinking of silence, of God, and of how she could live His Word.

She had been living for herself, mostly. And by herself. She interacted with Munir, with Upalu, and with Zahra, but did she really forge a meaningful bond with any of them?

Had she ever forged such a bond?

She was no longer sure, and her thoughts turned to Morgiana, who had been kind to her, and Shirin, who had taught her, and the vanished Sultana, who had had a smile like a rose.

Ninety-eight women had died before she had married the Sultan. Her life was spared, as if by a miracle, but it was so dearly bought. And how did she spend that life?

She prayed to God, who created man from a blood clot. Please, God, the Brilliant, the Strong, the Merciful, show me the way.

When the prayer was over, Dunya did not yet feel ready to join the city of Al-Rayyan. She lingered in the mosque, thinking and trying to reach God.

When she left the prayer hall, there were men sitting and talking in the foyer. One of them she recognized as the imam, who had led the daily prayer. He stood up and greeted her. She bowed to him and, without looking in his eyes, said, "Thank you for the prayer. It was very good."

What else could you say to an imam? But he continued the conversation, saying, "Thank you. I have not seen you in our congregation before."

"I am wandering through the city," she said, this time resolving to bite her tongue before she made any mention of the Palace.

"And why are you wandering?"

That was rather forward of him to ask, but he had led such a good prayer, Dunya felt he deserved an answer. "Because I want to understand the people, and how they live and think." She bowed her head further. "It was in a story I heard once." That excuse for all her wanderings sounded flimsy and hollow now.

"You have freedom," said the imam, "and an abundance of time to call your own. Seeking to understand others is a good use of those gifts."

"What do you know of people?" Dunya asked, looking up at him. "What's your story?"

The imam, a man in his sixties with hollows under his grey beard, was visibly surprised by this. "That is quite a question to ask a strange man you have just met."

"I ask as a student," Dunya said, hurriedly, hoping she had not given offense, "I want to understand, and praying here has only revealed to me how little I know. It seems that all I can gain is what I learn in stories. And so, in humility, I ask to learn something from you."

The man stroked his beard. "Are you on pilgrimage? It is quite traditional to trade stories on a pilgrimage."

"I don't think I am."

"But you say you are a wanderer. What do you wish to learn? Asking good questions is an important step to wisdom."

Dunya paused before answering. "When you look out at Al-Rayyan, what do you see?"

"I can answer that," said the imam, addressing his shoes. He sat and gestured to Dunya to do the same. "When I look at Al-Rayyan, I see much suffering. I see people who are afraid, because the officials are unjust. I know there must be a reason for it, but my eyes are turned to the people. And there, although I see fear, I do not see despair. I see wives getting up early to spin flax and make bread, and I see husbands working hard to bring home food and smiles for their children. I see people, not particularly learned, not particularly good, nor particularly bad." The imam sighed and spread his hands. "I see a world created by God—but a world fallen with human sin. I see a world that needs care. That is what I see."

Dunya listened, and could not think of a worthy response, so she got to her feet and said, "I have to leave now. My sister will be waiting for me. Thank you so much for your answer."

"I hope it proved helpful."

"You have given me much to think about," Dunya said. And then she left, pointing her shoes towards the Palace again. She did not cross the river that day, but returned to the Palace well before sundown. She went to the harem and took out a chess set. She arranged its pieces on the carpet and thought about Al-Rayyan.

"What is a city?" she wondered. "A city is a gathering of people all living together."

She went to the dining hall, ate supper, and returned to the Sultan's chambers. It seemed to her that the stories drew her like a magnet pointing to true north, and for the first time she wondered if that tyranny was worth the wonderful stories.

She was glad to find Zahra there, alone. "Hello," Dunya said in a small voice. "I'm sorry for speaking brusquely to you."

Zahra smiled, and it was equal parts maddening and comforting. "I've been called much worse."

Dunya laughed. She clambered onto the bed beside Zahra, and took off her headscarf. "I wanted to thank you for this gift. I've taken great advantage of it." "Tell me," Zahra said.

"I've been wearing it when I go out into the city, and I swear there is magic in it. I always find my way right back to the Palace when I wear it, and nobody notices me unless I wish to be noticed. I have learned much, going out into the city, especially today." She paused and looked down at the bedspread, embroidered with pomegranates and turtledoves. "There are people in the city who won't refer to the Sultan out loud. They treat his very title like a curse."

"And you treat his name like a curse," Zahra added gently. "His name is 'Sayyid.' Not 'the Sultan.'"

"Well, I—I—he's not well-known to me. I meant, I don't know him, so why should I call him by his real name?"

"To help you. You should not be so afraid of him."

Dunya had nothing to say to that. "My scarf—I mean, your scarf—it allows me to see what is hurt in the city and needs help."

"And what do you intend to do about that?"

"My life has been spared as though by a miracle—and more than that, I am now highly placed in the world. I intend to make a better use of these gifts."

Once upon a time, in India, there lived two sisters. The elder of the sisters married a woodworker, whom she loved deeply. The younger dedicated herself to caring for their parents. In time, the elder sister, named Shashi, grew heartsick and sad, for she wanted a child.

One day, the younger sister, named Priya, heard a woman in the marketplace hawking dates that could cure any sickness. Priya went to the street and asked the dateseller if her fruits could cure a longing for a child.

"Not my fruits, no," said the woman, "but I've heard that far to the east, between a green mountain and a white one, there is a valley where plenty of ginseng grows, and that root, harvested from that soil, has the power to make a woman conceive a child. But Allah alone knows."

Priya told her sister, Shashi, of this miraculous root and then she told her parents. With their blessing, she arrayed herself with three bracelets and journeyed to the east, searching for a valley between a green mountain and a white one.

When she crossed into the land of high mountains, she heard of war in the countries beyond. She sold one of her bracelets and purchased men's clothes, and, braiding up her hair, she disguised herself as a man. It was ill fate that she did this, for within three days of her disguise, she was assaulted while leaving a house of prayer. She awoke to find herself in barracks, among soldiers, and Priya grew afraid and prayed to God to protect and preserve her.

Her disguise as a boy grew more difficult to maintain, but maintain it she did as the army marched east. Rumors grew that they were approaching a valley of magic, and that kings and rajas of surrounding kingdoms wanted to take that magic for themselves.

Priya learned to fight, but took no joy in it. Her regiment came to a skirmish, and she survived only by the grace of God. Little joy she took in the bloodshed. In a fog of weariness she buried her slain comrades, while her commander spoke of glory.

The regiment came to a village of farmers, and stole and looted them at sword-point, even on the very doorstep of winter. As they left the city, Priya dropped one of her gold bracelets in the sand, hoping that a farmer's child might find it, that it might make the least amend.

They entered the country of China. In the distance Priya could spy a green mountain and a mountain that might have been white, or merely covered in snow.

The winter grew worse, and the regiment had no food and no money to buy any. Priya ventured out of the warm camp and to the nearest village, where she sold her last bracelet for some rice and onions. She was hailed as a hero when she returned to camp, but she was sorrowful, for now she had no way back home.

Spring came, and the armies moved to take the magic valley. The night they made camp, Priya crept out into the dark to search for the ginseng root, for she had every fear that it would be crushed in the battle which was to come.

The moon was full. She searched and searched, and prayed, and searched some more.

The earth shook and stirred under her feet. A dragon rose from the earth, glimmering silver in the moonlight, and it said to her, "I am the guardian of the river that runs beneath this valley. What do you seek?"

Priya spoke in her own voice, then, for the first time in many months: "I seek the ginseng root that will let a woman have a child."

"I can show you to that root," said the dragon, "but I will require payment."

"I have given all of my bracelets away," Priya protested, but she calmed herself. She had the measure of this dragon at once, and knew that he would not be swayed by pity. She said, "My first bracelet I sold to buy men's clothes. Without it, I would never have become a soldier. My second bracelet I gave away to feed hungry strangers, and my third I sold to feed my comrades-in-arms. Would you take the blood from my heart?"

"That would be an acceptable payment," responded the river guardian.

Priya took out a knife and cut the spot on her arm where her bracelets once hung. She cut only a little, without flinching, and the dragon drank up the blood and declared it satisfactory. A ginseng plant sprouted at Priya's feet, and she dug it up with her bare hands.

Then she hesitated.

Should she leave now, before the battle started, and head west, towards home and Shashi? Or should she stay with her comrades in arms, who did not know her true name but knew her courage? Could she leave them to fight without her? But could she abandon her quest for her sister?

"What do you think she did, my Lord Sultan?" Zahra interrupted her own story to ask.

"I think she turned around and left. She couldn't help it, it would be her nature as a woman to flee," the Sultan said without hesitation.

"As it so happens, my Sultan, she stayed."

Priya kept the ginseng root close to her heart, but she fought alongside her brothers-in-arms, and watched while the peaceful valley was covered in ruin. Her commander won the day and bragged that his name would live forever. Priya knew that the dragon below the valley would drink richly in the nights to come.

She stayed to help bury the dead, and then she turned her boots west, to cross the mountains again and go back into India. With her soldier's training and grim eyes, she had a safe crossing of it.

When she again crossed the threshold of Shashi's house, her sister did not recognize her until Priya pressed the ginseng root into her hands. Then Shashi cried aloud, wept, and hugged her sister around the neck. Priya had been gone for over a year.

Less than a year after Priya's return, Shashi delivered twins, a boy and a girl, and she named her daughter Priya.

However, Priya's peace had been shattered by her memories of war. She stayed long enough to see the healthy presentation of her niece and nephew, but then she departed their little village, saying she was going to seek wealth by trying her luck among dragons. She did not return for a long time, not until Shashi took up her staff, travelled to the dragons, and brought her sister home.

The Princess

A month later, Munir sent a request to Dunya to meet him in the Lotus Garden in the evening. She and Upalu arrived bright and early. Dunya sat uneasily on the edge of a fountain and occasionally had to warn Upalu off from setting the flowers on fire.

"I can't help it," said Upalu. "This time of year makes me so sad. It was about this time a year ago that..." she sighed.

"That you lost the girl who broke your heart," Dunya said. "Yes, I remember."

"I wonder if she ever thinks of me," Upalu plucked off one flower petal. It began to singe, and soon smoke drifted up from between her fingers. "Ever. At all. Even if only to be mad at me."

"I really thought you had forgotten her."

Upalu shook her head, and said no more.

"Ah!" said Dunya after a pause. "Here comes Munir."

Upalu gave a "Hm" and stood to attention. Munir and Hussein strode towards them, and Dunya saw that the Captain's head was bowed and his eyes were sad. Hussein stopped just out of earshot, but Munir stopped before Dunya. After he greeted her formally, he sort of slumped a little further and said, "Dunya, I've come to say goodbye."

"Goodbye?"

"The border wars are finished for now. Now we're building a trading outpost on the site of our old camp. I'm going to oversee the building of it."

"Must it be you?" Dunya asked, and bit her lip. Those were the words of a little child, not a Princess like she hoped to be.

"I know the project better than anyone—I should, I'm the one who proposed it to the Viziers five years ago. I was not sorry to leave the Capitol then, but I am now."

He reached out, and Dunya slipped her hand into his. There was silence, then Munir said, "There is no place for me here."

"Of course there is," Dunya said.

Munir didn't answer.

Dunya turned to Upalu. "Help me, here."

Upalu regarded Munir levelly. "Come to me when you know what you wish," she said. Then, with a little bow, she moved out of earshot.

"What do you wish?" Dunya asked Munir.

He didn't answer. After a pause, he asked, "What responsibilities do you have?"

That took Dunya aback. She cleared her throat, and said, "I...I am responsible for myself...and Upalu. She has no place in the Palace except as my lady-in-waiting. Of sorts."

"That's something."

Dunya's next words were halting. "I…if I don't keep an eye on Zahra, who will?"

"The Sultana? I should think she is watched at all times."

"But…I need to keep a particular eye on her."

"So you have responsibilities. Duties. As do I. But believe me," he gave her hand a squeeze, "I will return. Write to me?"

"Yes." Dunya looked down. Munir pulled his hand out of hers, and he crossed to Upalu. In a voice that carried—just barely—to Dunya, he said, "I wish that Dunya continues to be safe and happy."

"Funny," Upalu said, "I wish that, too. I'll do all I can to ensure it."

They nodded to each other. Dunya was still sorting out how she felt about this exchange, as Munir bowed to her and left. She watched him leave and sighed. He would come back. She had to have faith in that.

"Come on," Upalu said, taking Dunya by the arm. "Let's go to the harem."

As they started to walk, Dunya said, "You wish that I'll be safe and happy? Of all the things you could wish?"

"Munir and I both. He has a little good sense, after all."

"I didn't think…well."

"Well, what?"

"Sittou—my grandmother—was the only person I was really sure loved me. You two seem fond of me, too. I don't know what to make of it."

Upalu's arm grasped Dunya's a little tighter. "Take joy in it," she said. "That's my advice."

When they reached the harem, Upalu halted at the door. Dunya turned back to look at her. "What is it?"

"I should tell you," Upalu said, "Djinni live a much longer time than humans do—especially if they are sealed up in lamps, or rings, or whatever human sorcerers can devise. When my heart was broken, I was...well, I was mired in selfpity because I thought I would be brokenhearted for the rest of time. I was wrong about that. I, I don't know. I am better now. But you, Dunya... well, I will miss you for a very long time. I'm sure of that."

Dunya didn't know what to say. She held out her hand. "Come on," she said. "Let's get some dinner."

Dunya already knew how to read and write. Now she taught herself a new skill: how to forge handwriting.
Specifically, the handwriting of Sultan Sayyid.

After Munir left, the Palace seemed dreadfully quiet, and the city seemed full of strangers. Now when Dunya went into the city, she did not wander for pleasure. She sought to understand the problems of the people, from root cause to final consequence.

By investigating in the Demon Market, she found the nasnas mirror-merchant that she had met many years ago and spent hours listening to him talk of troubles with tariffs and the fickleness of the market. She visited the mermaids who were still living by the Second Gate and learned a little bit about the river traffic problems, but she learned more by actually paying a few captains for their time and listening to what they had to say. She spent hours in the cafés of the theater district, sipping coffee and asking the coffee merchants their thoughts. Thus she gathered the opinions of one class of people, and it was a frustrating day when she realized she had not spoken to anyone of a higher or lower class than "merchant." Oh, well, she lived with it and every day started again.

When she spent days in the Palace, she did not pass the time idly. Either she read her way through the economics and geographical sections of the library, or she sat in the harem and worked out the problem with the chess sets that the harems' occupants had left behind.

A month passed this way. By Dunya's tally, her life had been spared for a year and six months—some five hundred nights, give or take. Zahra told stories about a boy who climbed mountains, and the stories were thick with danger and fear, but the boy kept climbing, trying to reach the door of Heaven and knock.

Gradually, Dunya took more and more courage from these stories. There was a mountain for her to climb that seemed terrifying, and it was this: if her ideas were to do any good, she needed to communicate them to one of the Viziers. And the Vizier that she had the best chance of convincing was the one she least wanted to speak to: her own father.

She knew he enjoyed passing time in the Lotus Gardens, a place that Dunya did not want to go. It held more memories for her now. But it was the best place for her to talk to him.

She dressed herself as befitted her station, and with Upalu trailing behind her as attendant she headed to the Lotus Gardens. There she approached him.

"Father," she chose to address him as such this time.

He turned to her. "Dunya! It's been a long time. What do you want?" He gave her a discomfiting look. "You never speak to me usually, so I assume that you want something."

"I want you to listen to me. I have been going into the city, lately, and I have been doing my best to study the troubles of the people—

"I have been thinking of what might improve the lots of the people in Al-Rayyan. I want to share my ideas with you."

"Why not with the Sultan? You spend enough time with him."

"He doesn't care about the people of the city. You…well, you might."

"Thank you for your overwhelming confidence."

"Father, if you may remember, I have little reason to suspect you truly care for the lives of those under you."

Upalu leaned forward. "You're sounding angry," she whispered in Dunya's ear. Dunya worked to calm herself, but this did not do her much good.

"What, just because I gave you and your sister in marriage to the Sultan? Not that you ever thanked me for that."

"When I was brought to the Palace, every woman who married the Sultan died," she said.

Her father made a "Ssh" gesture, and looked around nervously. "Don't remind people of that. But it's all turned out well, hasn't it?"

"You're looking very angry," Upalu whispered.

Dunya composed herself. "You say I should put more trust in you. Then, will you do this for me? Will you listen to my proposals and implement them if they will help the city?"

"I will," he said. "You may not believe me, but everything I have done, I have done for the good of the city. You think you know its inner workings, and you can help it, fine, share your ideas. God knows we need a new perspective."

Dunya bowed. "Father," she said, "I ask for nothing more."

Her father brought her words into the Vizier's Council. Dunya wished for a way to listen, and Upalu picked up a lamp at random from the harem's collection and said, "Here, hold this to your ear." When Dunya did, she could hear the meeting between the Viziers and the Sultan, and hear her father reading out her own words. She smiled, thrilled to hear this, and rejoiced when the Viziers decide to adopt some of her suggested changes.

She resumed going out into the city, seeking to learn all that she could.

And somehow—she never quite found out how—the word got out that the new voice in the Vizier's Council chambers was the voice of the young Princess Dunya. Courtiers looked at her differently in the dining hall. They took notice of her, and Dunya did not always like their attention.

But out in the streets, when she listened to gossip under her blue headscarf, Dunya heard her own name mentioned from time to time, and more and more she was called "the people's Princess."

But she didn't want people she met to realize that they were talking to a Princess, so she called herself Rashida, these days when she went out.

It was a long and busy month for her, which turned into a year of new ideas and new ways of thinking.

She continued writing letters to Munir. She talked over and over with Upalu about the meaning and usefulness of courage and of pragmatism. And she listened to Zahra's stories.

Zahra announced that she was expecting another child.

The doctors set the delivery date at mid-August, when the summer heat would be torturous. Zahra again was at the center of a round of doctors and attendants to ensure the birth of another healthy child. As for Dunya, she was determined, this time, to pay attention. When the calendar turned to August, she and Upalu joined the throng of attendants on Sultana Zahra. And Dunya whispered to Upalu a wish: "That I may only fall asleep when I wish to."

Upalu whispered back, "That's a strange wish, but I'll grant it."

The wish was granted. On one particular day, Dunya felt a change in the air. She recognized it. She pretended to fall asleep, and lay down in the shade of a carved screen. Through a crack in her eyelids, she saw the other attendants fall asleep and lay down where they were standing. Even Upalu curled up like a flame banking to embers.

Only Zahra remained awake. And she picked up her veils, turned, and was gone.

Dunya sat up at once. "Zahra?" she said, at normal volume. There was something supernatural about this sleep; she needn't worry about awakening anyone. She went to where Zahra had been standing and rubbed her hand on the tiled floor. It was cool. In the August heat, that was remarkable by itself.

She waited. And she waited. The sun had begun to set when there was a cool breeze through the room, and a flutter of black cloth like a wing, and Zahra appeared. She hurried out of the room of attendants, and to a small side chamber, meant for washing. She took the ewer of water, poured it into the basin one-handed, and then Dunya heard splashing. Zahra was washing something.

"What are you doing?" Dunya asked, coming around Zahra's shoulder.

The older woman exclaimed in surprise. "Don't sneak up on me!" she chided. "You'll wake the baby."

Yes, there was a baby in Zahra's hands. This one was not colored blue, but he coughed up a storm. Dunya got a whiff of smoke. When she put her hands into the water, the water was nice and cool.

"I see you have given the Sultan another son," Dunya remarked.

"You are not to speak of this to a soul, you understand," Zahra said, washing the baby with great focus. .

"I won't," Dunya said. "Not even Upalu. Just like the first child."

For a time, there was silence, except for the splashing of the water and the child's coughs, which gradually subsided. Finally, Dunya asked, "Did you rescue him?"

"What?"

"Did you rescue him from a fire? He's coughing, he smells like smoke..."

"Yes."

"How?" Dunya gripped Zahra's wrist gently, so as not to hurt the baby, but she hoped to make Zahra look her in the eyes. She failed. Zahra remained focused on the baby. "Are you an enchantress? A sorceress? A pari? You must have magic in you somehow, I know it. You vanished…"

"It is not yet the time to tell you," said Zahra. "And you must make your peace with that, little sister."

Dunya let go of Zahra's wrist. She stayed by the basin, watching the little baby. When Zahra finished drying the child, she wrapped him up and handed him to Dunya. "There, make yourself useful. Remember—not a word."

Then, quick and silent as a shadow, Zahra returned to the main chamber and lay on the bed, just as the attendants began to come awake. One by one, they came fully awake and spoke to Zahra about what a wonderful, easy birth that had been, and what a handsome baby—oh, a second son, God be thanked in His heaven! Dunya handed over the child and having caught Upalu's eye, they left.

They went to the harem and played chess while the day cooled down. When the announcement rang out over the Palace— "Our Highness has a second son! All pray for the health of Prince Hashim!"—Upalu captured Dunya's pawn and looked up at her.

"There's something you're not telling me."

"Mm."

"You're barely paying attention to the game."

"Mm."

"It's something about Zahra. The baby. It had something to do with enchantment, didn't it?"

Dunya, her head leaning on one hand, looked up. "I promised I wouldn't tell anyone."

"That's as good as saying yes! What is at the bottom of it?"

"I wish I knew. I'm sorry, I can't tell you."

"I told you everything about me."

"But this is not about me. This is about Zahra. I barely know her, it turns out."

"Well, make a move. I stand to check you in about five turns if you don't start paying attention."

"Upalu?"

"Yes?"

"I'm glad you're my friend."

There was silence. Upalu finally cleared her throat. "It's not bad," she said, "being friends with a human. But you live such a short time. I try not to get too attached." And she did not capture Dunya's pawn. And that's how Dunya knew that Upalu was also glad they were friends.

There dawned a bright day in Syria, when the king announced that whichever of his three sons could catch a unicorn and return it to the court would be crowned the king.

This announcement spread across the kingdom. And in one tanner's shop, a girl by the name of Batel heard the news, and her eyes glinted, for she was as full of ambition as the shop was full of stink.

She said to herself, "I bet I could catch a unicorn, and a fair bit quicker than any of the princes. If I brought a unicorn to a prince, I could name my price—up to his hand in marriage. And so I will." That night, she scrubbed the stink off of her hands and slipped away, to seek a unicorn.

Batel had learned at her grandmother's knee three things about unicorns:

They are blindingly white, and to touch one would burn your hand off;

They are pure and like to live in the deserts and in the calderas of volcanoes;

They are intelligent and can speak any language, but are usually caustic.

Armed with this knowledge, Batel set out for the mountains.

She heard that the mountains closest to the sea hid volcanoes in their heights. Batel went to the merfolk that lived along the coast and offered them any service or skill they would ask for, if they would give her a means to ascend to the mountaintop.

The merfolk wanted a score of wineskins, and a score more of leather sacks, treated to resist water. Batel agreed, and the merfolk took her down into the water.

She swam around the base of the mountains and got as close as she could to the lowest volcano. Then the mermaids gave her precious shoes of fishes' mail and warned her that they would only last three days, so she had better find her unicorn quickly.

Batel lost no time in climbing.

The mountain air was sulfurous, but she was no stranger to fumes. The stone burned, even through her shoes of fishes' mail, but she kept saying, "And so I will, and so I will," and kept climbing. When she reached the caldera of the volcano, she could glimpse something white on the far end.

Then she unhooked from around her neck the cord of half-cured leather she had brought with her. She held it out, and tried not to breathe too much smoke.

As she had hoped, the unicorn was lured by the smell of the leather, the smell of death and feces that clung to it, because unicorns purify whatever they touch, so what is impure holds a great fascination for them. This unicorn sniffed Batel, close enough to scorch her hair, and she flung the cord around the unicorn's neck, and although the terrible beast snorted and stomped, it could not escape the touch of a virgin who had captured it honestly.

Batel pulled the unicorn down to the sea, but it fought her the entire way. It took a long time, but the sight of the sea frightened the fiery beast, and made it more obedient.

Calmer and with a clear conscience, Batel pulled the unicorn along the coast, and walked inland with it. As soon as the quenching sea slipped from view, the unicorn grew wild again, and she pulled and fought and yanked until her hands were bloody and blistered and she came into view of the glittering camp of the eldest prince.

This prince and his retinue were shocked at the sight of the unicorn, but gladly welcomed Batel when they saw she had it under control. The prince gave her a gold purse and promised more upon their safe return to the palace. Batel was happy.

Night fell, and the camp gradually went to bed, but Batel, who was still holding the unicorn's cord, could not let go of it, even tie it to a stake in the ground, because the unicorn would escape otherwise. Batel therefore stayed awake even when most of the camp fell asleep. At midnight, the unicorn spoke to her.

"Did you not see the jewels glittering on the prince's armor? Did you not see the stuffed peacock and quail he served to his guests? I saw. This prince would bankrupt your city to feed his own appetite for glamour. He would make a poor king."

Batel thought it over, and, to her frustration, had to admit that the unicorn was right. She got to her feet, though she swayed with tiredness. The unicorn bewitched the guards to fall asleep, and the unicorn and Batel walked out of the camp.

The next day, they reached the second prince's camp. This time, armed guards surrounded them before they had a chance even to see the middle prince. He rode up to them on a thoroughbred, his sword out and his helm raised. When he saw that Batel had brought him a unicorn, he welcomed her into the camp and gave her a gold purse. She was happy, again, until night fell. She could not sleep, for she did not trust the armed guard that the prince placed the unicorn under.

The unicorn bewitched the guards to sleep again, and said to Batel, "You see the blades and swords glinting in this prince's company? He will use me as a weapon. He will be a king of warfare."

Batel thought it over, and decided she would not consign the unicorn to that fate. She got to her feet, and again she and unicorn walked out of the camp.

The next day, Batel was so tired she thought she was hallucinating when they arrived at the youngest prince's camp. Again, he was delighted to see a unicorn, and again, he gave Batel a purse of gold. Batel did not like this prince, and when night fell, she only listened to the unicorn out of politeness, for she had made up her mind.

"You saw the look in the prince's eye when he saw me, tied with a filthy leather cord? He likes to know that something so precious and rare is his to hoard. He likes to keep me a prisoner. He will be the worst king of all: one cruel to his own people."

Batel said, "I know that, and I resolved as soon as I saw him to let you go. And so I will."

She untied the cord from around the unicorn's neck, and was not sad when it reared and galloped away without saying good-bye. She set out in the opposite direction of the unicorn, hoping her three gold purses would take her far in the world.

But it was not to be. Batel had fallen asleep with exhaustion before the sun rose, and the youngest prince's company found her, and held her prisoner, as punishment for setting the unicorn free.

But when night fell, the ropes around Batel's wrists caught fire and burned off, leaving no harm to her. They tried to clap her in irons, but the iron burned the blacksmith, and not her. And when her prison tent turned to ashes around her, they finally regarded her as cursed and set her loose in the desert. Batel did not look back as she walked away from them.

When she returned to the city, she used her gold coins to purchase the wineskins and commission the waterproof sacks that she had promised to the merfolk. She delivered these items personally.

She gave the gold away to her brother's family and walked into the desert. Years later, two unicorns were seen there.

The Singing Tree

A year after the mermaids took up residence in AlRayyan, they left. They requested of Dunya garlands of water lilies from the Palace, as symbols of peace and friendship. Dunya complied, but her heart was heavy when she and Upalu brought the flowers to Second Gate.

"I thought that you were happy here," she told Strength.

"It is not a bad life," Strength replied. "Our clan has never lived in a city before, and there is much to be said for it. The amount of garbage that comes through this river— mmm!" he smacked his lips, and his whiskers wriggled. When Dunya laughed, his smile disappeared. "But there is something in the water here that we do not like."

"Is it that sickness that you spoke of? I mean, that your leaders spoke of?"

Strength shook his head. "It is not only that. There is another spirit living in the river water, and it does not like our company."

"What sort of spirit?"

Strength gave a little wince. "We don't know. Even Rippleside, our wisest, can't knot up the nature of it in a few words. But we do know it's a spirit of death."

"You don't like death?" Upalu asked, over Dunya's shoulder. "But you eat all kinds of dead things."

"Excuse you!" Strength drew himself up haughtily. "So do you!"

"We do," Dunya agreed quickly.

"Death and decay are natural parts of the order of things, we know this better than anyone. But there is death, and then there is life-in-death, and that is what lurks in the Palace. That is what frightens us."

"And that is what lives in the Palace?" Dunya asked. Strength nodded, and would not say more on the subject. Dunya and Upalu bade him and his cohort goodbye, and watched as the mermaids swam away from Al-Rayyan, holding up the water lilies with pride.

"You know," Dunya said some time later, "I thought I was doing all right."

She had ordered coffee and pastries, and she and Upalu were sitting in the harem, talking about their place in the world.

"I thought," Dunya went on, "that, alright, the Sultan is a very bad man. Yes, he might kill my friend Zahra and then myself any day now, but I was getting used to it. He—you know, he annoys me more than anything else these days. He barely has patience for his own children, and every day he snaps over some petty little offense. But I thought that the terrible illness that the mermaids Winterborn and Waterfall-Climber mentioned—I thought maybe I had managed that illness all right. And now along comes Strength to tell me there is some kind of cursed thing in the water of my Palace. And it's as though all the work I've done doesn't matter at all."

"It matters," said Upalu. "The people in the city seem better off with a few of your reforms in place."

"But not enough."

"You sound ambitious."

"Perhaps I am. Perhaps I am a little ambitious. I was never made out to be a wife, after all." Dunya twisted the cloth of her robes in her hands, "But I am a politician's daughter. But what do my reforms matter if the Palace's water is poisoned?" She sighed. And she thought. And finally she said, "Maybe it's the river spirit." "The who?" Upalu asked.

"The spirit of the river Rayyan, the one who made the contract with the people of the city years ago. It was a story my grandmother told me…and I told the merfolk…the point of it is, the river promised to be gentle and strong for as long as the people on the river were generous, giving shelter to the stranger and stories to the wind."

"And garbage to the river, I assume." Upalu's voice was dry.

"Well…the mermaids liked the garbage, didn't they?"

"They sure did."

"But that wasn't enough to keep them here. Maybe it's…oh, I don't know! But the spirit of the river may know what the life-in-death spirit is. I need to find it and talk to it. But how?"

"Leave Al-Rayyan."

"What?"

"You heard me. Leave the city. Travel to the source of the river. The spirit of the spring water should do."

"I can't leave Al-Rayyan. I can't leave Zahra's stories. Don't narrow your eyes like that!"

"Just how wonderful are these stories? They never seem that special when you try and tell them."

"That's because I'm not the storyteller that Zahra is."

"She's a mystery."

"I know, I know. But—can it really be that the spirit of the river Rayyan lives in the spring, in its source? Then how could she make a contract to form a city here?"

"I don't know." Upalu shrugged. "I avoid water whenever I can. But don't rivers usually have more than one spring that feeds them?"

"That makes sense..." Dunya stared out the window. Upalu went on.

"I know this will be hard for a girl like yourself to hear, but, well, when you live as long as a djinni does, you realize that very little that a human does really lasts. Even the wildest wish granted by the strongest djinni will only last for so long. Human beings are like bits of wood, eaten up in the fire of time. But the history that they make, that is like a river. Many little springs, flowing together to make one great course. And that course itself can be altered by mountains, by stones, or by people themselves. Oh, this is a poor metaphor. Dunya, do you understand? You must not try to carry the world upon your shoulders. Dunya…you're not even listening to me!"

"A spring," said Dunya. "Maybe there is a spring in the city that feeds the river—and maybe the spirit of that is what struck the bargain, long ago. And maybe, a spirit so old and knowing, maybe she will know how to heal the city." Dunya got to her feet. "I have to go. It's time for Zahra's stories."

"Oh, resist their call for one night!" cried Upalu. "Just so you know your life doesn't depend upon them!"

"But Upalu," Dunya paused by the door of the harem, "as far as the Sultan's concerned, my life does depend on them." As she left, Dunya heard Upalu mutter, "Always have to have the last word."

She hurried up to see Zahra, and was relieved to find the older woman alone—that is, without the Sultan present. The two little princes and their nursemaids were there, and Zahra laughed and played with the children. Dunya hung in the doorway and watched them.

She is not their true mother, thought one side of her.

But she rescued them from death. Didn't she? thought the other.

It's clear to be seen that she loves them. Loves them more than the Sultan does. Look at her smile. That makes her a true enough mother for me, thought a third part. And presently Zahra dismissed the attendants, saying it was time for the Sultan to arrive. She gave little Hashim's foot a last tickle, and then when they left, she stared after them.

"What are you wondering?" Zahra asked aloud.

"I'm wondering how much you care for the children," Dunya answered.

"I care for them very much. They're darling, aren't they? But what are you really wondering?"

In brief, Dunya explained her concern about the river, the river spirit, and the possibility of a spring somewhere in Al-Rayyan—possibly several springs, she added, considering the number of little neighborhood wells.

Zahra listened to her, and when Dunya had done talking, she closed her eyes. "Before the door to the baths, but beyond the garden of spices, there is a door of dark wood. This door leads to the wine cellar, where things that must be kept dark and cool lie. Within this cellar is another door, and beyond that door there are steps that lead down, and down, and down below the castle, to a reservoir that holds a spring that feeds the river." She opened her eyes. "There is a spirit that lives there. But beyond that, I cannot tell you."

"It must be the river spirit," said Dunya. Behind her, she heard the door open and the Sultan step in. Dunya slid to the floor, by Zahra's knee, and without looking behind her she said, "Sister, would you please continue the story you started last night?"

Now she felt the pull, between the part of her that sat still and listened to the stories, and the part that wanted to follow Zahra's directions and seek the river spirit in the dark.

That morning, when the story ended on another cliffhanger, Dunya went to bed and dreamed again of the space below the Palace, where the water was littered with jewels and someone was crying.

The next day, she found Upalu and told her where they were to go.

With that, they dressed for an adventure, with hardy, practical trousers and shoes and blouses. Dunya brought a torch, which Upalu lit when they descended into the first cellar. It was easy to find the first door, harder to find the second. But when they reached the third door, Upalu stopped, and when Dunya looked at her, the djinni shook her head.

Upalu was very pale. "I can't go down there," she said, in response to Dunya's unasked question. "I can't. You know what water does to fire."

Dunya finally nodded. "Very well, then." She turned.

"But I'll be here when you come back," Upalu blurted out.

"I'm glad to hear that," Dunya said. Her hand pressed the threshold of the doorway, and she passed through.

The steps were straight, at least; Dunya gave thanks for that. Her little torchlight illuminated the stone walls. The passage was narrow and every so often, Dunya's feet slipped on a puddle. She never fell, but her heart pounded in fear that she would.

Finally, the steps widened out, and the passageway opened.

Something was there before her. Dunya lifted her torch, but couldn't make anything out beyond a shadow. A man's shape, taller than her.

"Who's there?" she asked, at the same time that a lower voice asked, "Who goes there?"

Dunya was silent, dearly tempted to say, "I asked first," but also aware that it would be a bad idea.

"Who goes there?" the shadow said again.

"Dunya," she said. "Princess of Al-Rayyan."

The shape came a little clearer—the shadow-man was holding a spear. He looked, Dunya thought, very like one of the Palace guards. Maybe he was some kind of magical protection. He said, "Hold out your hand."

Dunya held out her hand, trying not to wince. She expected a blade across her palm at any minute, but instead the shadow said, "Your hand is clean. You may pass," and stepped aside.

Dunya passed by him, cautiously, and was almost overwhelmed by the sense of sorrow that radiated from him. But the man had vanished out of sight when she looked again—she didn't get to ask him anything.

Finally, the reservoir appeared before her, a flickering floor of water. Dunya found it fascinating. She had never seen so much still water in her life. She lowered her torch.

A cry broke the silence, and Dunya jumped, almost dropping her torch.

"What are you doing here?" demanded a strident voice.

"Who is it?" asked another, at the same time.

"It's not safe here! Leave! Leave!" cried a third.

"I wish—I wish you no harm!" Dunya cried as the water sloshed about her feet. "I wish to talk to the spirit of the Rayyan River!"

Another cry, a gasp, and laughter. "The Rayyan River!" One voice repeated. "Why are you seeking it here?" Asked the second, as the third wailed, "It is long since gone, gone, gone."

Dunya lifted her torch. "I wish you no harm," she repeated, "But if you are not the Rayyan River, then who are you?" She listened as hard as she could. There was something very familiar about the voice's accents, if she could only place it through the echoes...

"I have no name," said the first voice, "and I have no home here."

"Coming here may have been your death," said the third voice.

"Who are you?" Dunya cried.

"I am—" And what followed was a cacophony, a chorus of voices speaking all at once, different words, and Dunya couldn't make any sense of them.

After the echoes had died away, Dunya said, "I don't understand."

The voice wailed at that, wailed so terribly that Dunya almost dropped the torch to cover her ears. "I don't understand!" Dunya screamed over the wailing. "Are you a ghost? Are you a water spirit? Tell me!" she hollered at the top of her voice.

Was it her imagination, or was the noise in the chamber softer just a bit? The wailing stopped, but the echoes went on, and when the echoes finally died away, Dunya's ears rang so hard that she almost didn't hear the spirit say, in a chorus of three voices, "You mock us. "

Something was in the water. Was it moving, or—no, that was just the firelight. Dunya raised her torch, and the changing light gave clarity: it was a root system. Roots were spreading through the water. Little ones like capillaries at the water's edge, growing bigger and thicker as the water grew deeper. And they grew out from something to her left.

Dunya stepped to her left, and when the tree came into the light she jumped—it almost looked like a person. But it was a tree, a stunted little tree, hardly her own size, with a smattering of leaves. "How did a tree grow down here, so far from the sun?" Dunya asked.

"We don't need sunlight," said the ghostly voice. The first voice.

"We have other food," said the second.

"Please, leave, it's not safe for you here," the third said.

"You're the tree?" Dunya asked.

For a moment there was silence, then a keening wail, joined by another, and another. The leaves of the tree began to shake. Dunya brought her torch closer.

"No closer!" shrieked the three voices at once. Dunya drew back—but she'd seen what she needed to. On that wretched tree, every leaf had a face. A woman's face. And the leaves were keening.

"The Sultana's dowry gift. The Singing Tree." The torch started to shake in Dunya's hand. "But that tree was cut down. I saw the stump of it. You are…you can't be…"

"We can't be what?" asked a voice—Dunya thought of it as the second voice.

"Trees don't have ghosts."

"Clever," murmured the first voice.

"Put the pieces together," said the second.

"All living things have a spirit," said the third.

"I will find a holy man," Dunya said. "I will get you freed. See you put at peace."

"Peace!" Three voices screamed. "There is no peace without justice! Justice!"

Dunya hollered over the echoes, "Justice for what? Where did you come from?"

"Blood," came the answer, horribly low and earnest. "The blood of ninety-eight women, murdered in hatred, murdered without justice. A little blood seeped its way here, to the darkest shadows…a little blood from each woman, so a memory of each woman lingers here."

The murdered harem, Dunya thought. Terror clawed at her mind, but she would not give it the upper hand. She said, "I'm—I'm talking to ninety-eight ghosts?"

"Ninety-eight remnants. Ninety-eight memories. Ninetyeight prayers of fury. The souls have gone; Allah alone knows where. The anger remains. We remain."

Silence fell. The echoes died away. Dunya stared at the little tree, clutching the torch with two shaking hands. She said, "I pity you, with all my heart I do. But…What should I do? The water…"

She was going to say, You are poisoning the water, but her mind worked quickly, and she saw it wasn't true. The Sultan was the one poisoning the city. The Sultan, unbounded in his power, the Sultan who had acted with such cruelty to those under his protection.

"Tell us," begged the third voice, "You who come from the sunlight…"

"Tell us you will do something," said the second voice.

"Tell us you have some courage," said the first voice.

"I…" Dunya tried to think of any action she could take, something she could do, but nothing came to mind. Talking wouldn't work. Listening wouldn't work. Nothing but dark water, and paths that ended in her own death. "I…I don't know."

There was a sound like a great inhalation and then, a scream, not three screams at once, but ninety-eight. "Justice!" they howled. "Justice!" They repeated, stretching the word so loud and long.

The third cry of "Justice!" shook Dunya to her bones. She dropped the torch. It fell into the water and guttered out.

She would not scream. She would not panic. She backed up until she hit the wall. "I am not afraid," she said, "I am not afraid." The stairs were to her right. She would simply sidle to the right and pray not to fall into the water, pray that her memory had not failed her.

She felt overwhelmed with sadness. She had reached the shadow guard, which meant the door.

She fell through the door and raced up the stairs, not knowing if she was imagining the sensation of cold hands around her ankles. She ascended, and didn't stop until—

The firelight of the wine cellar. She fell to the flagstone floor and gave God thanks for fire and deliverance.

"What happened? You look awful…" Upalu was there, and she picked Dunya up with surprising strength and gentleness. "Let me take you someplace safe."

"Away…" Dunya said, in what was almost a wail.

"Yes, away from here." Upalu didn't ask any more questions until they reached the harem. There she snapped her fingers and called up a blazing fire, and Dunya, lain by the fire, started to warm up at once. "Did you see the spirit? Was it the Sultana's ghost?"

Dunya winced at the word "ghost," and realized something else. The guard who had emanated sadness, was that the Sultana's lover?

"The singing tree," Dunya said. "The singing tree that was the Sultana's dowry-gift…it was cut down, but…there's another one growing down there. And it's…I don't know that it's a ghost, but it's a remnant of something. Near a hundred ghosts, a mosaic of ghosts, something from each of the women the Sultan killed."

Upalu whistled through her teeth. "That's a bad omen if ever I heard one."

Dunya shook her head. "My ears are ringing."

"What happened to your torch?"

"I dropped it."

"Well, it's gone. You're never going back there." Dunya was silent.

"Dunya, you have a knack with supernatural things, but this is way beyond you." Upalu knelt by her. "You stay away from that pool, you hear me? So there's a—whatever you want to call it, a multi-faced ghost hanging around. That's as clear an omen as ever you could ask for."

"An omen of what?"

"That it's time to leave."

Dunya sat up. "What? Leave? Leave the Palace?"

"Leave Al-Rayyan. The city follows how the King goes, and the King's Palace is a cursed place, from its rooftops to its foundation. It's time to leave; nothing good awaits this city."

"But Al-Rayyan is my home! I can't leave it!"

"What? People leave their homes all the time. It's called growing up."

"But Zahra…"

"If I have the measure of her right, she'll be fine whatever happens. People like her have a way of profiting no matter what."

"No, Upalu, I can't leave. Al-Rayyan is my home."

"You did your best by it. But now it's time to move on."

"I won't," said Dunya. "I can't."

"You can," Upalu corrected, "but you won't."

There was a pause. "Will you leave?" Dunya asked.

Upalu was a long time answering, so long that Dunya blurted out, "Don't leave me. Be brave and stay with me. Please?"

Upalu narrowed her eyes, and raked a hand through her hair. Smoke billowed up and her eyes sparked. "I'll stay for

now," she said finally.

"Thank you." Dunya reached up to the djinni and gave her a tight hug. "I don't know what I'm going to do now. But I won't run away."

That resolve was sorely tested the next time Dunya saw the Sultan.

Sayyid, she thought. His name is Sayyid. I must get used to using it.

They were listening to Zahra's newest story, Dunya with only half an ear. Her mind was with the Sultan. What could she do, to appease that spirit that dwelt in the reservoir? Could she somehow make the Sultan see the error of his ways, and resolve to be a better man?

Dunya couldn't think of a way how. She wanted to believe that some good dwelt in him, but he had murdered ninety-eight women who relied on his protection and care.

She couldn't look at him anymore. He might see the fury in her eyes, hear how her breath was coming fast and her hands were bunching into fists. It was new, this feeling. She was furious with him. I am not the one who should help

him,

she thought. Why does it have to fall to me? Why does

everything fall to me?

And her conscience piped up and said, Because you are the one who

chooses to act.

But what do I do this time? Dunya thought. And she didn't have an

answer for herself. For the first time the roads outside of Al-Rayyan beckoned.

It was terrible. It was worse than hearing about storms, or the terrible Roc,

king of the skies, or forty thieves concealed in oil jugs. Sitting there beside him

almost completely defeated Dunya's nerve, but she kept thinking, I must be

brave. I must remain, for my city. For my city. For my city.

Dunya found her eyes straying to the windows, more and more often. She

jumped when she realized she was lost in contemplation of leaping out the

windows, landing softly, and running.

Dunya was the first one to spot the sun rising in the east. When she did, she

heaved a sigh and rubbed her forehead, listening again with half an ear as the

Sultan told Zahra that she would finish the story in the next night, but first, he

would get some sleep.

Thank God Dunya thought, going to her own bed, but she did not sleep. The voices of the singing leaves were still ringing in her ears, and she twisted this way and that, until finally—

She jumped when the door opened. "Dunya?" asked Zahra. "What is the matter?"

Zahra sat on the bed beside her. "What is disturbing you?"

In a rush, Dunya told Zahra about her visit to the reservoir, with her words falling over each other. She was very tired. "It's worse than an ordinary ghost, Zahra. An ordinary ghost is just the spirit of one person, but this is the spirit of ninety-eight women, all of the women that—" Dunya swallowed. "Zahra, we have to do something."

"Perhaps a holy man," Zahra said. "Don't people usually call holy men at times like these?"

"I'm afraid that this spirit will only be appeased by—by the Sultan's actions, and Allah knows I can't get him to do anything. But you could, —surely you could get him to…" "What can I do? What influence do you think I have over him?"

"Your stories…"

Zahra said nothing. Dunya sighed. "We have to do something to get that…that thing out of the reservoir. It's evil…"

"No, the spirit that you speak of is not evil," Zahra said firmly. "They may not be human, but ghosts seek justice above all else. If you must revile them, reserve a little pity for them, at least. Dunya, I know that you were married to the Sultan."

Dunya stared at Zahra. That marriage had been so long ago, she herself had half-forgotten it. For so long, having Zahra in the place of the Sultana had been just so much better, Dunya hadn't thought…Now she listened.

"You have a choice, though. You can leave Al-Rayyan. You do not have to remain in his household. Leave now, and
I will pave your way so that you are forgotten and free."

"But my city," Dunya protested. "My city needs me."

Zahra smiled. "You really are a daughter of Al-Rayyan," she said, "ever giving. Well, sleep now. You need it."

Dunya slept an unusually long time that day. She woke up and began to form plans.—I'll get Upalu, we'll head to the Demon's Market, then I'll find that kind imam and we'll go from there, and then she realized, it was already late afternoon.

Dunya could not remember the last time she had slept so late. She bolted out of bed, dressed herself in a hurry, and ran towards the harem, her blue scarf in her hand.

By the entrance to the harem she stopped and looked around. The stump of the miraculous singing tree had long since been dug up. A few roses grew there now, noticeably smaller and younger plants than those around them.

The singing tree had been magic made tame. Now Dunya was dealing with magic poisoned, or gone rotted, or somehow gone wrong.

"What will I do?" she sighed. She crossed into the harem and stopped. Something was different. She looked around. The curtains were drawn back, and the scent of smoke that clung to Upalu was gone.

"Upalu?" she called. And that's when she heard heavy footsteps and realized the other thing wrong. All of the lamps were gone. There were no lamps scattered on the floor or neatly arranged on tables. The only light was from the sun—all the braziers were gone, as well.

The source of the footsteps came into view. It was a man, a member of the Sultan's personal guard. Dunya felt a chill of remembrance. This man had also been a wedding gift, part of the squadron of soldiers from Ethiopia. "You," he said. "You're the Princess?" "Y—yes," Dunya managed to say.

There was a pause, and the man said, in an undertone, "Get out of here. Now."

"You hear someone?" came a call from an adjoining room.

The soldier talking to Dunya turned towards the voice. "I didn't hear anything," he said. "Told you, this place is haunted." He caught Dunya's eye. "Go," he mouthed.

"My friend," Dunya said. Her fist tightened around the blue scarf in her hand. "Where is my friend?"

"I don't know," he whispered. Then he turned and walked away, seemingly unconcerned.

Dunya backed away and found herself outside the harem. Don't run, she thought. If you run, you draw attention to yourself.

"Where would she go?" Dunya twisted her scarf, then, in a decisive motion, set it over her hair. She set off in the direction of the Palace kitchens.

The kitchens were as busy as ever. People jostled past Dunya when she headed towards the fireplaces. But the first fireplace had no djinn there, nor the second, nor the third.

"Upalu!" Dunya resorted to standing on tiptoe and calling, "Upalu!" But her voice barely even carried over the yells of the head chefs, and no one looked her way.

She grabbed some food and headed for the workshops. Maybe Upalu had taken refuge in a forge. After the workshops, Dunya sought out the library. Upalu had never gone there, for fear of starting a fire, but maybe? Who knew?

Finally, the Lotus Gardens. No luck. Dunya sank onto a bench. The sun was low, and golden light got into her eyes.

Is she in the city? she asked herself. I'll just go to the Demon's Market and come right back, she promised herself.

She got up and hurried to the main Palace gate.

There was so much foot traffic, it took her longer than usual to get to the Demon's Market. When she got there, her feet steered her to the one place she knew where djinni liked to congregate: Upalu had said she liked the café, once, on a bright winter day.

The café was full of hookah smoke and the aroma of very strong coffee. Dunya shouldered her way into the room and looked around for a cinnamon-colored scarf, and then looked again, praying for a friendly face, anyone who might help.

And no one did. Why would they? She was invisible.

Dunya hesitated. She considered flagging down a server, but thought, what would she say? She left, and realized that the stars were coming out.

Dunya swore by everything she could think of, and resolved she would check just one more café, and then return to the Palace.

Three cafés later and she still hadn't found her and there was an urgent voice in her head screaming at her to return to the Palace. So she turned back towards the Palace, whispering, "I'm sorry, Upalu," over and over.

The moon was bright and shining when she finally reached the Sultan's suite. Standing before the door were two of the Sultan's personal guard, as inscrutable as ever. It was so late.

Zahra can't start the stories without me, Dunya thought, pulling down her blue scarf. What if... what if...

She stopped between the two guards. Dunya laid her palms on the door. She felt—what did she feel? Reluctant. She thought, I don't want to do this. I don't want to keep living through this charade.

"I have to," she muttered, and pushed the door open.

Zahra was on the bed—the worst had not come to pass —and the Sultan was pacing.

"There you are," Zahra said. "Come, sit by me." "Where were you?" the Sultan asked her.

" The kitchens. I was hungry." Dunya sketched a curtsy.

She had almost reached the bed when the Sultan asked, "Why do you spend so much time in the harem?" When Dunya turned to him, he said, "I do keep an eye on what happens in my Palace. What's in the harem for you?"

Dunya glanced at Zahra. No help forthcoming. Dunya said, "I, um, it was where my father first brought me. There are…memories."

"Memories. So you're a bit sentimental. That's sweet, in a young lady."

"Husband," said Zahra, "come sit by me."

"I don't feel like stories tonight," the Sultan commented. A shock went through Dunya. Zahra's smile froze. "Now, the harem," he said, "A beautifully designed area, I always thought. The screens, the cushions—the chessboards. I was there just earlier today. There was a chess game in progress. The players were gone." He turned and fixed Dunya with a half-smile. "Do you play chess against yourself?"

"Yes," was the prompt reply. "I do. I'm the best opponent I know."

"So no one passes time in the harem with you?"

Dunya said, "No, I'm quite by myself."

"You know what else the harem has in abundance? My old aunt used to collect them—brass, copper, tin—" "Collect what, dear?" Zahra asked.

"Lamps, of course."

Lamps. Djinni. Upalu. Dunya's hands clenched around the sheets. Be calm, she thought, Don't give anything away.

Where is he going with this?

"As those lamps are technically mine now, I took the liberty of confiscating them." His eyes glanced up, gauging Dunya for a reaction.

She cleared her throat. "As is your right."

"I will have them destroyed in the morning. The smiths are already notified."

"That is also your right." Dunya forced her hands to relax.

The Sultan stepped closer to her. "I wonder what I'll find," he said, "when they're all melted down?"

Upalu would have looked him in the eye and said, A lot of hot metal. Dunya felt very keenly that she was not Upalu.

She bit her tongue.

"What...will...I...find?" Sultan towered over her.

Zahra, help me, Dunya thought desperately, but Zahra was silent.

"You won't find anything," Dunya said at last. "There's nothing to find."

"Nothing? Then how is it that a squeaking little nothing like yourself manages to grab so much power? Charm? Beauty?" He barked a laugh. "I got the idea from listening to Zahra's stories. Which number was it? Perhaps number sixty? Or six hundred? My head is stuffed with the damn things. I'm hardly good for anything now but stories. This one is so old it creaks. The motherless daughter finds a djinn, wins its loyalty with kindness or her pure heart or— some contrivance. She somehow comes to marry a prince and rule the kingdom. Well, I don't like that story much." Dunya's breathing was coming very fast.

"This much I know: You have a djinn somewhere. Does it live in one of the harem's old lamps? An earring of yours? Anything is possible." He leaned back a little. "By rights, you should already be in irons, for conspiring against your lawful Sultan. But I'll strike a deal. Tell me where the djinn is and I'll forgive you this ambition. But the djinn comes to me, or I will take it by force."

"And wish?" Dunya asked. "You'll make wishes, I suppose? What more can you possibly want out of life?"

"Of course I'll make wishes. What a stupid question. What, if my wishes are sufficiently pure of heart, you'll hand the djinn over?" He paused.

"No." Dunya was half-surprised by her answer.

"No, you don't care if I'm pure of heart?"

"No, the djinn is not yours. She's not mine to hand off."

"How noble of you." He stepped away and took a few strides across the room. Dunya for the first time saw something on the floor—a large circle, drawn in chalk, with triangles and radiating lines within it. Dunya herself stood on the edge of the circumference. The Sultan went on, "I'm going to give you one more chance."

"Or else?" Dunya's voice came out higher than usual. "Or else you'll kill me? Like your first wife?"

In two strides he crossed to her and struck her, hard, across the face.

"Dunya!" Zahra cried.

"There's your chance," the Sultan hissed through his teeth. "Now you'll see how I punish usurpers."

"You kill them," Dunya said. "It's not hard to figure out."

The next blow struck her eye. Footsteps hurried to her. Zahra's cool hands were on Dunya's shoulders, helping her stand. "You're out of your mind," Zahra said to the Sultan. "There are no djinni here."

"Not yet. Step away from her, wife." The Sultan waited. Zahra didn't move. "I said, step away. You are helping a traitor and usurper to my throne."

"She's not even fighting back," Zahra said.

"And why should she? The djinn will come when she truly has need."

Dunya's panic rose, but she beat it down. She thought, I won't call out. I won't give Upalu a reason to come here. I won't. I won't.

"Show mercy!" Zahra's hands tightened on Dunya.

The Sultan didn't answer that. "Dunya," he commanded, "Daughter of Shareef. Call the djinn."

Dunya turned towards him and spat on the floor.

The Sultan moved quickly, so quickly. He seized Dunya's hand and wrenched her out of Zahra's hold. He took her arm, twisted it, and pinned her against the wall. Dunya bit her lip as pain exploded in her shoulder. He increased the pressure, and the world in Dunya's eyes started to go red. Her only clear thought was, I'm going to die, I'm going to die, I'm finally going to die.

And abruptly, the pressure stopped. The hands on her arm released her. Dunya took a few deep breaths, and turned to look.

Was it—had she hit her head? Was her good eye playing tricks on her? The Sultan stood there, his eyes unfocused, arms and legs as limp as an unused marionette. Zahra's hands were passing over him, she was working magic.

"Let it not be said," she muttered, "that I have no sense of mercy. Upalu."

'How do you know her name?' Dunya asked just as a column of flame materialized to Dunya's left, outside the circumference of the chalk circle.

"Dunya!" the djinn cried, regaining her human form.

"It's not safe for her here any longer. Take Dunya away." Zahra's tone was a command.

"But my magic—"

"Is safer than his wrath. Go."

Dunya felt Upalu's arms around her, and then the arms turned into fire.

Fire surrounded her, out of nowhere, with no spark or source. The fire took a hold of her, and Dunya was brought up and carried in a whirlwind. She knew Upalu was with her.

In her fear, that was enough. Upalu was taking her away.

The heat was terrible. Dunya covered her face with her hands in a moment of self-preservation. When she caught glimpses between her fingers, she saw streets below her. They were moving very fast, ascending by the minute. Dunya squeezed her eyes shut and said, "You're burning me."

"I'm sorry," replied the flame, and cold desert winds broke through, enough to keep Dunya from burning.

How long they traveled, Dunya never knew. Maybe she passed out. She came to again, on a sand dune, and slid downward before coming to a stop. Upalu's hands were tearing at her. "Your robe!" she exclaimed. "Wake up! Help me!"

Dunya realized her outer robe was on fire. She shuffled it off as quickly as she could. The burning cloth soon lay in a heap on the sand. Dunya realized her blue headscarf, Zahra's precious gift, was burning, too. Unthinking, she leapt for it, but Upalu pulled her back. Dunya's strength ebbed. She sagged in Upalu's arms.

The djinn scanned the horizon. "Where is he?" she asked.

A cold wind brushed over them. Dunya shivered. "I'm cold," she muttered.

"Don't be afraid."

The sound of hooves approached. Dunya looked—her eyes were caught by the thousands of stars high above— and there, in the distance, lay a large camp. Coming close to were two horses, bearing men, and the first man— "Munir?" Dunya asked.

"About time," Upalu muttered with relief. She laid Dunya on the ground and crouched by her.

Munir's horse shied; Munir dismounted and ran towards them. "Dunya, Upalu, what are you doing here?"

"She's hurt," Upalu said. "You have to help us."

"Of course," Munir said. "Help me get her onto the horse…"

"Horses don't like me," Upalu said. Munir picked Dunya up.

"Gently!" Upalu urged.

"She's burning up…" Munir, after setting Dunya on his horse, looked at Upalu and asked, "Can you follow us?"

"Yes."

"I saw—I saw fire land here. —What are you?"

"I'm a djinn," Upalu said. "We should have told you before."

"It's all right." Munir mounted his horse and said to his companion, "Hussein, ride ahead and alert the medical tent." He clicked his tongue, and his horse began to walk, turning back towards the lights of camp, at a pace that was steady but didn't hurt Dunya.

Dunya lolled her head back. "So many stars," she mumbled.

"Yes, it's very pretty, isn't it?" Munir said. "Keep talking, Dunya. Stay with us now."

A gleam of light behind them caught Dunya's eye. She looked and saw Upalu, brilliant and fire-wreathed, leap into the sky and fly onwards towards camp.

"So that's what she really looks like," Dunya said, slurring a bit.

"We'll get you someplace safe in a moment," Munir said. "Just keep talking."

"Keep talking. Stay alive. That's a story I know."

"You don't have to worry about a thing."

Softly, Dunya said, "I'm not worried. You two are looking after me."

Part Three

The Desert

There are perils of traveling with djinn in the shape of fire.

When Dunya was brought to the medical tent, she had a raging fever. Munir called for the head medic to tend to her. As she was lain on a pallet, Upalu arrived in human form again.

"Where did she come from?" asked the head medic.

"Al-Rayyan. Of course," Munir replied. His face was bloodless and drawn.

"In the middle of the night?"

"It was an emergency. I had no other choice." Upalu fretted as she watched Dunya. "If she dies from the fever, I'll never forgive myself."

"Both of you, out," said the head medic. "You're not helping. Wait outside."

So they went outside of the tent, regarded each other warily, and waited. Munir sat on the ground, and Upalu paced to and fro.

In the tent, Dunya passed in and out of consciousness. The candles of the medical tent flickered, and the head medic ordered the brazier's fire built up. She sighed gladly when he laid a cool cloth on her forehead.

"Thank you, Sittou," she murmured.

"You're welcome," replied the head medic gruffly.

Dunya tried to focus on him. It wasn't her grandmother; he was only half of a whole shape. He was a nasnas. No, now he had scales and whiskers--a merman. The fire dimmed for a moment, and for Dunya the shadows deepened. She heard the sound of trickling water. And the sound of keening cut into her ears...

"I tried," she said to the tree in the reservoir. "I tried, but what can I do? I tried, I'm sorry, please, leave me!"

"There, there," said the medic. "Drink this. It will be all right. Rest."

Dunya drank the medicine he offered and drifted off. But her sleep was uneasy. The keening noise followed her through arabesques, mosaics, and the little warren of rooms that had belonged to her grandmother.

Things grew clearer—she was back at the feast, the Sultan's wedding feast, and she watched as the singing tree was presented by the bride's father. The tree grew out of its pot, and put down roots in the banquet hall. The guests continued to laugh and toast, and only Dunya could see how the roots were tangling into everything, burrowing, snarling, choking— She had a moment of clarity—she was in an unknown place, a tent, and there was a glow of sunlight through the cloth. "Where am I?" Dunya asked.

There was no one there to answer. Then she appeared: her hair falling in a wave of silver and black, her face lined with the ghosts of many smiles. But she wasn't smiling now.

"Morgiana," Dunya said, and reached for her. But her shaking hand passed through Morgiana, as though through mist.

"You are in Captain Munir's camp," Morgiana said to Dunya. "North of the city. Recover, but don't take too long." "I have not forgotten you," Dunya said.

"Then help me," said Morgiana. "Help me." Roots twined up her throat, around her hands. Leaves grew from her hair.

Then she was gone. Dunya called her name, but there was no returning apparition.

Dunya slept deeply. The next time she awoke, her head was clear and her fever had broken. She lay there, in the sunlight, for some time before the head medic entered. "Ah, you're awake," he said. "How are you feeling?" She managed a small shrug.

"You must be hungry. I'm Dr. Samaq. Captain Munir and that young woman will be very happy to hear you've woken up."

"The young woman?"

"Strange sort. She doesn't seem to need to sleep, but she eats like a fire..."

"Upalu," Dunya said happily. She settled back.

"Are you curious as to where you are?" asked Dr. Samaq.

"The camp—I mean, maybe it's a town now. The one on the borderlands."

"A town in progress." The doctor bent down and examined Dunya's black eye. "On the mend," he said. "I'll get you something to eat."

"Can I see my friends?"

"Yes. But sit back. Rest. Rest," he said, scowling until Dunya lay back again.

"Yes. Of course." Dunya struggled to sit up, until the doctor told her to rest. He disappeared through the tent flap, and Dunya had a moment to take in the strange new setting.

The flap opened and Upalu came in, followed by Munir, ducking under the low ceiling.

"You're awake! I was so afraid." Upalu knelt by Dunya and clasped her hands. "It was my magic that cast the fever, I was so afraid, but the Sultan would have killed you

.Are you well?"

"I'm fine," Dunya answered.

Another medic, not Dr. Samaq, entered with a plate of bread and herbed olive oil, setting it down beside Dunya.
She took a bit of bread and realized she was ravenous.

"Get your strength up," Upalu said to her. "What was happening in the Palace?"

"Where were you?" Dunya asked. "I looked all over for you. The kitchens, that café you like—the harem was being raided."

"Yes. When the Sultan entered the harem—it was late morning, I think—I knew it was time to leave. I waited by the First Gate, I waited for you, but you didn't show. I was about to leave when something summoned me to the Palace."

"I didn't. I wouldn't have…"

"Was it Zahra, then? I don't understand. What was happening?"

Munir said, "Upalu told me that she saw you with the Sultan and Zahra, and the Sultan was threatening you, so she took you away."

"Not only that, you forgot," Upalu chided him. "There was an arcane circle on the floor."

"The chalk circle?" Dunya asked.

"That's the one. The Sultan has been reading up. He wanted to bind me."

"That's…exactly it," Dunya admitted. "He somehow figured out that there was a djinn in his Palace. He confiscated the lamps of the harem because he thought you lived in one of them. And he was trying to…" Dunya raised a hand to her black eye.

"Beat the truth out of you?" Upalu asked sharply.

"He wanted me to give up the power of the djinn. I said that you weren't mine to hand over. And Zahra intervened. She said something—did something to the Sultan. She enchanted him, turned him into some kind of puppet."

"Could…could she do that all along?" Munir asked. "Why didn't she do that earlier?"

"I think Zahra was the one who summoned you," Dunya said to Upalu.

"Well, then," Upalu nodded, "I'm grateful to her. And now we are out of Al-Rayyan—which is where I wanted to be —and we're all fine, and we can just stay in this camp. Right, Munir?"

"Absolutely," Munir replied at once. "You are my honored guests. You can stay here, make your home here, if you want. I won't say it's the same life you're used to, but I would be glad to have you here."

Dunya kept eating bread with oil, and didn't say anything.

"But first," Munir said to her, "You will rest."

Dunya left the medical tent the next day. The desert wind whistled in her ears. The camp had its noises to be sure—the pounding at the smithy, the goats and horses braying, the conversation everywhere—but beyond that was a profound quiet. It was the silence of the desert.

Upalu helped her through the camp. At her approach, goats leapt away and horses whinnied.

"Oh, shush, you," she would say to all of the animals.

There were structures going up, but most of the camp's residents remained in tents, and it was a tent that Upalu had conjured up with magic. It was stationed close to the medical tent, just in case, and colored a warm orange, like banking embers. The men and women who had lived at the camp a longer time glanced curiously at the vibrant newcomers, but neither Upalu nor Dunya paid them any mind.

The tent was a little barren on the inside, but it had carpets and braziers, sleeping rolls and kitchenware. "Did you conjure all this up?" Dunya asked her friend.

"Munir provided the furnishings," Upalu admitted. "He says they were surplus. My magic isn't limitless, you know." After Dunya settled in and had changed into new clothes —clothes that didn't smell of smoke—Upalu said, "Well, come on, we've got to go to market."

"Why? What do we need to buy?"

"Not to buy. To work. Would you rather rest, though?"

"No, no, I'll come with you."

Dunya followed her to the market in the center of the camp. Upalu explained to Dunya that while the hall of justice was still being built, the marketplace served as the center of government, such as it was. "Munir asked me to help out. Can you guess why?"

"Because you've become friends in my absence?" Dunya asked.

"No. Well, kind of. But look around."

Dunya looked. They were passing by the forge. Dunya looked in the forge, and saw men toiling at work with the flames, except— "They're djinni," Dunya said, pausing to watch the one smith with fire curling around his arms.

"Very good. And over there?"

Dunya looked. The workers trading jokes as they laid foundations for a building—they had goats' legs.

"Satyrs?"

"Just the same, from pretty far west. There are even a couple of mermaids who have set up shop in the river bend. People have been leaving Al-Rayyan in droves, and some of them came here."

"Is that so," Dunya said. Now that she knew what she was looking for, the camp had more than its fair share of not-quite-human folk. She tried not to stare.

Upalu went on, "But the ifrits want a better share of land, and Munir wants a…what would you say, an interpreter, maybe, or just someone to smooth out the negotiations. Hence, me."

"That's wonderful," Dunya said.

"It was my idea," Upalu said, as they ducked to enter a large tent. People were seated in a circle on carpets. Munir sat opposite the door, and on his right side were six ifrits, ranging in appearance from enormously tall and horned to petite with the whiskers of a tiger. Upalu bowed to them— Dunya followed her lead—and they sat in the space provided.

Dunya listened to the negotiations with half an ear. She observed how well Munir listened, how seriously Upalu took her task. She smiled with pride at her friends, and thought, So this is a growing town. A new town, without even a name yet. Maybe I can live here, and be happy.

It was strange getting to sleep that night. The tent swayed in the wind, and though the inside was nice and warm thanks to Upalu, the night winds snuck in every so often. When Dunya closed her eyes, she was back with the djinn, traveling through the sky like a comet, trapped in fire.

It took Dunya a long time to fall asleep, and when she did, she dreamed vividly.

She dreamed that there were footsteps sounding just outside the tent flap. When Dunya peeped outside the tent, she saw a woman in a rider's outfit, looking up at the stars.

"Shirin?" Dunya asked.

Shirin turned and met Dunya's eyes with a long-gone, sardonic smile. "Well met," she said. "Getting better?"

"Slowly," Dunya said. She got to her feet. Shirin looked well, but she did not smile.

"Is this a dream? Are you a ghost?" Dunya asked.

"Dream. Vision. Visitation. What does it matter?" Shirin waved a hand—a hand encased in a thick leather glove.

"A falconer's glove!" Dunya exclaimed. "There was a story about you and—and a princess who could turn into a falcon. It was so romantic, and…"

The look on Shirin's face made her stop. She had never seen Shirin so sad, so defeated.

"It's just a story," Shirin said.

"But it was…" Dunya trailed off. "I'm glad to see you."

Shirin half-smiled at that. "Thanks. You've grown up well. I wanted to see you. I was always sharp-tongued, but I hope you never took it seriously."

"It's alright, really it is," Dunya managed to say. The wind began to pick up.

"Listen to me, Dunya. I am not resting well."

"I'm sorry to hear that, but what can I do about it?" Dunya begged. The wind grew stronger. A particularly strong gust made Dunya close her eyes, and when she opened them again, Shirin was gone.

Dunya woke up, and it was early morning. he could hear some people moving around outside and she shivered.

She kept this dream to herself. That day, Upalu took her to the edge of camp, and they sat looking out into the desert. At one point, Upalu said "Isn't the silence marvelous?"

The wind wailed in Dunya's ears. She shivered and said nothing.

That night, she dreamed of Morgiana again.

"It is good to see you," Dunya said to her. In this dream they were out in the desert, with the lights of camp small in the distance.

Morgiana didn't smile, didn't speak.

"Did you heal me? Did you help me to get better?"

"No, you are young and strong, and I had nothing to do with it," Morgiana said. "Dunya, did I ever set you at ease? Was I ever kind enough that it mattered?"

"Of course," Dunya said. "Of course you were."

"Then help me. Dunya, I am not resting well."

"I'm sorry," Dunya cried. The wind picked up, and oh, how it battered at Dunya, so that she had to cover her head and shrink to her knees, because if not…

She woke up that morning clutching her ears, and Upalu asked if she was all right. "I'm fine," Dunya said to her. "Just a bad dream."

Dunya kept this dream locked tight within her. That day, Munir took her to the paddock on the eastern edge of camp. He took out a cold-blooded mare and helped Dunya mount it, sidesaddle.

"You don't have to be scared. I think the horse likes you," he said as he led the mare around the paddock.

Dunya smiled tightly. "It's nice up here," she managed to say.

She was afraid to go to sleep that night. She tossed and turned, and hoped that she could make it to morning without waking up, but…

She dreamed of Zahra.

Zahra was wearing red, not black. She said nothing, only stared at Dunya with wide, mournful eyes.

"Are you dead?" Dunya asked her.

Zahra shook her head. Still silent. "Zahra? What do you want me to do?" Zahra said nothing.

"Zahra, what can I do? If I go back, I'll die. You can't ask me to go back."

"I'm not asking," Zahra said at last. Red beads appeared in a line circling her neck. They began to grow larger. A drop ran down to her collarbone.

Dunya covered her eyes and screamed, "I'm sorry!" She woke up to Upalu beside her.

"Dunya, Dunya," said the djinn, "It's all right, you were only having a dream. It's okay. He can't get you out here."

Dunya nodded, staring at the ceiling, listening to the wind.

The morning grew brighter. They walked around camp, and were cooking chickpeas for lunch when Dunya said, "I have to go back."

Upalu asked, "Back where? Back to the market?"

"No. Back to Al-Rayyan."

"No" was the first thing that Upalu said.

"I've been having dreams," Dunya cut her off. "They're getting worse. I have to go back."

"Bad dreams? Those are common to people who have had experiences like yours, violent ones."

"It's not—look, I think they're messages. From the dead."

"From the dead." Upalu stared at her.

"Yes. How can I leave that undone?"

"Very easily."

"Upalu. I have to go back, and I've made up my mind."

They kept arguing until a chickpea popped. Upalu suggested that they eat lunch. She ate very fast and excused herself. Dunya suspected where she was going. A while later, her suspicions were confirmed.

Upalu dragged Munir into the tent. "Munir," said the djinn, "Dunya has taken leave of her senses."

"Maybe I've come to my senses," Dunya said. "Listen. I've had dreams, dreams of the women that I knew that the Sultan killed. They aren't resting easy, neither Shirin nor Morgiana. And the last one was about Zahra. I can't leave her there, to whatever the Sultan may decide to do. She saved my life—twice, she saved my life."

"You might die if you go back there. Almost certainly will die," Upalu said.

Dunya swallowed hard. "Then I'll have had..." she tried to count up, "I'll have had a thousand good days, give or take."

"Help me out here," Upalu said to Munir. "What's the news from the city?"

"Not much." Munir admitted. "There hasn't been any word of the Sultan in a different mood than usual, but news can be slow to reach us. Dunya, please consider. Don't you have –" he gestured around him, "Don't you have a future to live for? A place? You can have a place here, you and Upalu. Life is a gift, you can't squander it."

"We're not meant to just live," Dunya said. "There's…" she hesitated, searching for the right words.

"I swear," Upalu said, "if you utter one word about Zahra's stories, I will…"

"The stories don't matter! This is about right and wrong. I can't leave Zahra to die. If there's anything I can do to get her out of there alive, I owe it to her."

"There might not be anything you can do," Munir said.

"By the sounds of it, she's fine," Upalu added.

Dunya took a deep breath. "I just have a feeling there's not a lot of time left. Anyway, I don't need your permission. I was hoping to have your help, but I'll go myself." "No," Upalu said at once.

"You can't," Munir said at the same time.

"What, will you hold me prisoner?" Dunya snapped at them.

"I—" Upalu stopped. Munir laid a hand on her shoulder. Upalu glanced back at him, then turned to Dunya. "I don't want to see you die, or hurt," she said. "But if you're set on this, then you will have my help."

"And mine," said Munir. "All I ask is…wait until we get news from the Palace. We may hear later today. Or we may

—"

"Captain!" Came a voice outside the tent.

"—Or we may not," Munir finished, turning towards the voice. "I'm here," he said, "I'll be there."

Dunya followed him into the blinding sunlight of day. The speaker had been a courier from Al-Rayyan. He brought with him dispatches, both verbal and written. Munir opened the Palace news at once. He scanned it, then read it again, and said to Dunya, "Zahra lives, but the Sultan has had her imprisoned."

"Imprisoned?" Dunya repeated.

"You're sure?" Upalu asked, emerging into the daylight.

"Read it yourself. It says that the Sultan has become wary again. It's a mood of his. I'm sure it'll pass," he added, as Dunya read over the dispatch. It had been written by one of the Palace Viziers, but not her father.

Dunya waited until Munir dismissed the courier. When they reentered the tent, he glanced sidelong at her. "I have nothing more to ask of you. But you have my help." "And mine," Upalu added.

"Where is she likely to be imprisoned?" Dunya asked him.

"There are a few likely locations..."

"Is the harem one of them?" Dunya interrupted.

"Yes."

"I'll look there. I just need a way to get back to AlRayyan, and I need spells to pass by unseen." She didn't have Zahra's blue scarf anymore.

"I can do that," Upalu said.

"Can you help me get Zahra out of the city and to this camp?" Dunya asked her.

"Absolutely. Easiest thing in the world."

"I have a question," Munir said. "Considering we will be harboring a fugitive wanted by the Palace, can your magic keep Zahra hidden for a long time? Or..."

"As long as you need. Djinn magic comes from the heart," Upalu explained. "Dunya? What's wrong?"

Dunya was covering her mouth and her eyes were scrunched up. "From the heart," she said. "Both of you, thank you." Before they could say anything, she reached out and hugged them both. She squeezed her eyes shut and wished she could hold this moment, and them, forever. I

shall have to make plans, she thought, 'In case I die. She

hugged them a bit tighter, and then let go.

It was three days of steady riding to reach Al-Rayyan. Upalu followed Munir and Dunya, in fire form, and joined them in the evenings.

The sun was setting over the desert when they came to the walls of Al-Rayyan. Munir went to stable their horses and pay for fresh ones. Upalu joined Dunya, who was looking up at the walls.

"Zahra might be dead by now," Upalu said.

"She's not. I know it. Not yet," Dunya replied. She adjusted her headscarf—it was secondhand, from camp, like everything she was wearing, but she didn't mind. It would get her where she needed to go.

Munir rejoined them. To Dunya he said, "Do I need to go over the Palace plan with you?"

"No," Dunya said, giving him a smile. "You've gone over it enough. I know where she might be."

"And you know the ways out?"

"Yes."

"One last thing," he said. He reached into his belt and drew out a small knife, neatly sheathed. "Just in case," he said firmly, handing it to her.

"Thank you," she said. Then she clasped his hand, and said, "I'll see you soon," in what she hoped was a firm voice.

She turned to Upalu. "I'm ready. Let's go."

Upalu passed her hands over Dunya's head. Dunya shivered, remembering the spell, or whatever it was, that Zahra had lain on the Sultan, and then Upalu said, "It's done. Let's go."

With the djinn as a wisp of smoke, Dunya headed towards the First Gate and passed unseen under the eyes of the guard. She made her way to the Palace, never looking back nor to the sides.

When they reached the main gate of the Palace, Upalu rematerialized and said, "I can join you if you'd rather—"

"Just stay here, in case I call for you." Dunya smiled up at her. "And meet me here when we come out." "Of course." Upalu felt silent.

"I wish I could tell a good story," Dunya said. "A story of a courageous lady who finally found a voice. A story of direction, you know? Meaning." Dunya went on.

"We have the stories we're given," Upalu said, "but we can direct the way that they go." Dunya reached to clasp her hand, but Upalu hugged her tightly. "God be with you," she said. "I'll be here."

Dunya nodded and entered the Palace.

She headed southwest immediately, and felt a pang of guilt—she hadn't told her friends about this errand.

But she went to the garden of spices, and from there to the wine cellar, which was dark, and to the steps leading down to the reservoir, which was even darker.

"Should have brought a torch," Dunya remarked to no one. She shrugged and began her descent, keeping both hands on the wall of the stairwell. She was a long time going down.

She almost fell when the steps leveled out and she saw light at the end of the passage. Between her and the light, there was that shadow guardian again. Still standing at attention, looking as if he would never rest until the world came crashing down.

Dunya held out her hands as she approached him, and the guardian said, "Your hands are clean. You may pass."

She passed him, felt that wave of sadness again. She saw that the light was coming from the water itself, luminescence tinting the slightest ripple. The light was scant, but enough to see the tree by.

"I'm back," she said.

The tree began to sing, to lament. Dunya approached it, and felt pity for the stunted little thing. It should have seen the sun long ago. She knelt on its roots, ignoring the pains in her knees.

"I will do," she said, "whatever I can, to help your spirits rest easy. I swear it."

She could never quite account for what she did next, only that it felt right, as right as anything she'd ever done. She drew out the knife Munir had given her and held out her left palm. She winced preemptively, then drew a thin slice along her palm, as carefully as she could.

"Ouch," she hissed and flexed her hand so a little blood fell onto the tree, its roots. The leaves went silent. And then, there seemed to be close to a hundred little sighs, and the tree started to turn, leaf by leaf, into mist, into air.

Dunya got off of the roots, sheathed the knife, and turned back. She didn't need to see the end. When she reached the wave of sadness, she said, "I will see if I can help you, too," and started to climb up. When she reached the open air again, she went in search of Zahra.

The Last Story

She had told Munir and Upalu that she would check all the places where the Sultan kept prisoners, but she had a very clear idea of where the Sultan would keep Zahra.

So, she headed straight for the Palace harem.

It was heavily guarded, just as it had been when Dunya had first arrived at the Palace. Lights danced in the windows, casting patterns on the ground and walls around.

The guards did not cast a look at Dunya, which meant Upalu's magic still held. Dunya passed through the doorway, blessing the djinn and all magic that came from the heart.

When she passed into the main chamber, she saw the Sultan and Zahra arranged in a not-quite-familiar tableau: the Sultan was sitting at Zahra's knee, his eyes focused on her; behind her there was a delectable picnic dinner with pastries, cheeses, and a green bottle of wine.

Dunya stepped into the room and closed the door. The Sultan glanced at her, but did not interrupt the story. Dunya stood by a pillar. When Zahra finished the story, she looked up at Dunya. "I'm glad to see you," she said.

With that phrase, Dunya felt the go-unseen magic on her break away, like glass. The Sultan looked straight at her and said, "I wondered if I would see you again." He stood up slowly. "That was a good story, wife," he said to Zahra.

"You're not going to call for the guards?" Dunya asked.

"No. I only wanted them to bring you to me if they saw you. Well, somehow you got past them. You've got more brains than I gave you credit for. Here, have some wine."

"Perhaps you should abstain from wine, dear sister," said Zahra. She got up and embraced Dunya. "It's good to see you again."

"You can't possibly be finished tonight, wife," said Sayyid, after swallowing a morsel of cheese. "You had better come up with another story, if your head likes the neck on which it sits."

"Have you been all right?" Dunya asked in a whisper. "I came to see you as fast as I could." "Do not be afraid," said Zahra.

"But I am," Dunya replied.

"You do have another story, right?" demanded Sayyid.

"I do," said Zahra. "Why not have some more wine, husband, and I will tell you. Dunya, please be calm."

"Yes," said the Sultan. "If you came all the way here, you may as well enjoy yourself. I'll have you arrested in the morning."

Zahra laughed gently and sat back down on the sofa. The Sultan sat at her knee, with a wineglass at his hand, and Dunya stiffly sat on the bed.

"Once," Zahra began, "there was a princess whose hair was like gold and silver cascading down her back. Her smile was the smile of a rose, and her heart was as a lotus, overflowing and offering to all. Her name was Farizad." The Sultan almost choked on his wine.

Dunya kept her composure, but her heart began to hammer. Farizad was the name of the Sultan's first wife, the wife who had betrayed him, the wife who had always been kind to Dunya when she was nothing but a neglected daughter.

"Farizad had all the learning that befits a princess, she had all the graces that befit a woman, but she lacked one thing: parents who loved her. Her parents instead had a mind for fortunes, for titles, and for how much gold they could amass to line their coffins when they died. They sought to acquire more, unaware of the gift they already possessed.

"One day, a terrible creature came to their house. This creature promised the parents precious metals and as many titles as they could wish, if they would give him their daughter, with gold and silver hair.

"I am sad to say, the parents did not hesitate an instant before handing her over. Farizad's mother told her to bear the creature's wrath with grace; her father told her to bear sons.

"There was a grand wedding, but Farizad quaked when she sat beside her new husband, for he could…"

"Halt, halt!" the Sultan said. "I know this tale. She came to love the creature after seeing the way he tended to his garden of roses. With her love the spell came undone, and the creature was revealed to be a handsome prince. I am grown wise to your tricks, wife—you've told this story before!"

"This is not that kind of story," Zahra replied, her voice flat. Her eyes dared the Sultan to interrupt again.

The Sultan, taken aback, said nothing. Finally it was Dunya who, for one last time, asked Zahra to continue.

"The creature that had claimed Farizad for his bride was most terrifying, for only she could see his true shape. He had the power to disguise himself and take human form. To all others, he appeared the very zenith of courtly manners and valiant courage. He appeared, in fact, as a Sultan."

"What?" the Sultan exclaimed. But Zahra did not stop.

"Farizad toiled, day and night, to be kind, to be patient, to be obedient, as her mother had told her. She tried to calm her husband, to nurture some seed of goodness within him, but she was met with nothing but wrath and greed, and a delight in the pain of others. The people loved her, for she was kind to all, even to unwanted daughters, but the walls of her bedchamber echoed with weeping, more nights than I care to tell.

"One day an embassy arrived from an African empire. The empire was rich with gold, and its emperor was eager to forge alliances with other nations, especially those that heed the word of our beloved Prophet. To this end, he gifted a squadron of soldiers to the monster-Sultan as a token of friendship, delivering men as though they were animals. Twelve soldiers, drilled to perfection and brave as steel, became part of the Sultan's household. Proud of them, the monster made half of them his own bodyguards, and half of them his wife's.

"These soldiers were each well-favored, skilled with weapons, and clever. But one soldier, assigned to Farizad's protection, was kind-hearted as well. Over time, Farizad began to welcome him as a friend, and then fell in love with him.

"Despite their wisdom, the worries of Farizad's ladies-inwaiting, and the warnings of the man's brothers-in-arms, the two indulged in their love, seeing it as a gift from God, sent to relieve their sorrow. The exiled soldier and the miserable Sultana. But they were careless, and one night Farizad's husband, the monster, found them together. He raised his claw and—"

"Slew them!" the Sultan cried, getting to his feet. "He slew them like the animals that they were, the ungrateful swine, the scum of the earth! He granted her a clean death, better than she deserved! How dare you speak that woman's name in my presence? How dare you?" "I only tell the tale, your Majesty," Zahra replied.

"This is how it ends," Dunya whispered to herself.

"Well then, what happened to Farizad and the soldier? Finish this tale wrong, wife, and your head will be forfeit."

Dunya clenched her fists in her hands. She was not afraid of the Sultan; in an instant, she was only irritated with him for how petty, selfish, and temperamental he was.

But Zahra seemed not at all bothered. She contemplated the room a while and looked at Dunya, before turning calmly to the Sultan and answering, "I took them." Dunya was nearly as confused as the Sultan was. When he asked her to explain, Zahra said, "I took them. You cut Farizad through her heart and you beheaded the soldier, Chemharu, on the spot, and I took them away to where you could never hurt them again. That is as far as their story goes; I can tell no more. Sayyid, darling, why not have more wine?"

In the silence that followed, Dunya asked, "Zahra, who are you?"

The Sultan said, "The Sultana must not utter blasphemies."

Zahra looked up at him and said, "What blasphemy?"

"What blasphemy? It must be blasphemy, to lie to a Sultan, to tell him one distracting story after another, and for what? To save your head? And what do you mean, you took them away?"

"I was sent here," Zahra answered. "I was sent here by the Judge. I hovered long over this Kingdom, taking bride after bride. I took women who wept, women who forgave the men ordered to kill them, brides who dared Allah to claim their fiery souls. On and on, until the Merciful One sent me to you in this form, to stop the sacrifice, and see if my wisdom could calm your heart. You were right," she said to Dunya, "Time has run out for me." To the Sultan she said, "I stayed with you for one thousand and one nights—nearly three years. Every morning for you was a new chance, Sayyid. I hoped for your salvation. If your heart softened, my eyes would be keenest to see it. But, I grieve to say your heart is not calmed. I have been a loving, faithful wife to you, yet still you hold the sword above my head."

"But who are you?" the Sultan cried. Dunya, her soul filled with awe, had already guessed. Not a djinni, not a marid, not a spirit, not an enchantress—

something she had never thought of, that she should have realized from the beginning. She slipped to the floor and prepared to kneel, thinking, I was ready to die when I walked in here. I am

ready now.

Zahra's black veils lifted around her, carried up as if in a great wind, until they seemed to flap and stretch of their own volition. And the threads of silver in the black glinted, and the glints widened until they became eyes, blinking in the smoke of the brazier. Zahra seemed to grow taller and lovelier still, until the eye hurt to behold her.

"I am an Angel of Allah, the Watchful, the Judge," she said, "I am the Angel of Death. And I pass sentence upon you."

Dunya bowed to the floor, hiding her eyes. There was a roaring like a mighty wind, and a feeling of terror and awe and wonder. And then, empty silence. She looked up, and in a glance saw the Sultan stretched out on the floor. His eyes were wide and empty. Dunya shuddered to see him.

She reached over and closed his eyes. "You could have been better," she said out loud. "I'm sorry you'll never get another chance." Dunya straightened up and decided. She raised her voice. "Guards! Guards!"

The door opened, and the first duo of the Sultan's guards entered. They stared at what they saw. Turning, they yelled for reinforcements.

It seemed to take forever for the Sultan's guards to file into the room, and then to cross the wide empty space to the bed. Dunya remembered the story she had just heard. They were, she realized, the men who had lost a brother-inarms to the Sultan's wrath.

The Captain came forward, signaling to one of his lieutenants. The Captain of the Guard looked hard at Dunya, and then he studied the Sultan's body. The lieutenant looked at the wine glasses, and the green bottle that was almost empty.

"No weapon," said the Captain. "No markings." "No poison," said the lieutenant.

"Where is the storyteller?" the Captain asked Dunya.

She swallowed hard. "Gone," she answered.

She kept her chin held high. She did not want to die, but if that was the place God had chosen for her, she would accept it with grace.

The Captain signaled again to his lieutenant, who put the wine bottle down. The Captain knelt before Dunya, and his men followed suit.

"Young lady," he said, "You have been witness to a miracle. It is not every day that God strikes down the wicked in our own time."

"A miracle," Dunya repeated. It was agreement, and it was a new way to frame what she had seen.

The Captain went on, "We do not presume to know the workings of the Most High, but you have been given to us as a Sultana, delivering our lives from the horror of that man. We pledge our loyalty to you, Dunya-zhade, she who delivers the world."

She was without words. It took her a moment to remember her part in the story—and as they had said their part, she would say hers.

"I accept your fealty," she said to the Captain. "I thank you." She swallowed, the air was still, and then she said, "Well, we might as well get this over with. Please call the

Viziers, and bring them here."

The Vineyard

When the Viziers arrived, Dunya made a quiet exit. They would call for her when they needed her. In the meantime, in the adjoining garden, she called out "Upalu," softly.

Upalu appeared, a trail of smoke solidifying into a human form.

"What's happened? Why is it taking so long? Why—why is the spell on you broken?"

"Zahra broke it. She's gone now. And the Sultan is dead."

Upalu stared.

"Zahra broke the spell. She's gone back to where she came from, but not before k-killing the Sultan." Why did she stutter on that one word? Dunya squeezed her eyes shut. I
just saw a man die.

Upalu gripped her shoulders. "Hold on, Dunya. Hold fast. The Sultan is dead? This is a good day, then. Off to a good start."

"Yes," Dunya said, "Yes, it is. I want you to bring Munir here. Tell him what I've told you."

"Are you sure?"

"Yes."

"I can take you with me."

"I am not going to leave again."

"You'll be all right here?"

"Yes, I will."

"I'll be back as soon as I can," Upalu promised. Then, in a curl of smoke, she was gone.

At that moment, the harem door opened, and Dunya's father approached her. She had only seen him look so worried on the night before he had brought her to the Palace harem.

"Dunya," he said to her, "the Sultan is dead, and his other wife—that Zahra—has fled. What do you know of this matter?"

Dunya looked at him and felt no fear. "I know that she took him."

"She took him? Talk sense! His body is lying there stinking up the harem. Where did she go?"

"Honored father," Dunya said, "You would not believe me even if I told you."

Shareef simply stared at her. "She poisoned him," he said. "She poisoned him and fled into the night somehow. And you—you were not even supposed to be in the Palace. How were you in the harem tonight? The entire Palace guard attests that you were there, but they all affirm you are innocent."

"And I am."

"Then who killed the Sultan?"

"Zahra did."

"And where did she go?"

Dunya shrugged. "She was your daughter," she replied impishly. "Maybe you would know."

"My daughter? What are you talking about now?" demanded Shareef. "She was a courtesan. A woman of the harem."

"If you say so, Father."

Shareef sighed. He got up to leave, but Dunya grabbed him by the sleeve.

"What is it?" he asked.

"The children," she said, indicating Almas and Hashim. "They are innocent. You must promise they will not suffer for what their mother may, or may not, have done."

Shareef grunted an assent, and Dunya let him go. When he was gone, she settled herself down on a bench. She suddenly felt very, very tired, and it looked to be a long night ahead.

Dunya thought, By now Upalu will have reached Munir. Will they travel by fire to the Palace? Possibly. If not...

She might have dozed off for she was very tired, but when she closed her eyes, she could still see Zahra, her veils lifting and turning into wings.

This is not a comforting thought, Dunya admitted to herself.

And then her thoughts shifted, and she remembered what Zahra had said about being "sent by the Judge." The Captain of the Guard had called it a miracle. It was unmistakable.

Alone, Dunya composed herself and said a silent prayer. As she whispered, "Praise be to Allah, the Compassionate, the Merciful," her spirit was soothed. She was able to breathe deeply again.

"Dunya!"

"Small lady?"

Dunya finished her prayer in a quick whisper and opened her eyes. Before her, Upalu and Munir were hurrying towards her, from the main gates. Behind her, the Captain of the Guard had spoken.

She turned to address him first. "Yes?"

"The Viziers wish to see you."

She thanked him and stood up. She waved to Upalu and Munir in acknowledgment. The Viziers were lining up outside of the harem door. Behind them, the Palace doctor and his assistants quietly went inside, to tend to the body of the late Sultan.

Dunya brushed off her outer robe and addressed the Viziers. "I am here. What do you want?"

The oldest of the Viziers stepped forward. "On the advice of the Sultan's Guard, and our own counsel, Prince Almas must be crowned, but he is in need of a Regent. Would you take on this responsibility?" Dunya took a moment to compose herself, long enough for her to hear Munir and Upalu arrive behind her. Then Dunya stepped forward.

"I will," she said. And her future began there.

After the noon prayers that day, Dunya was crowned Sultana-Regent of Al-Rayyan. She gave a short address to the people from the high balcony. She promised them that she would uphold the law, protect the city, and respect the legitimacy of Prince Almas, when he came of age. The people cheered, and it was with a great sigh of relief that they settled down to an impromptu feast.

Dunya moved her things into the nursemaids' chambers, so as to be closer to the little princes. Her conscience pricked at her that she had neglected them of late. And besides, the Sultan's chamber was full of memories—overwhelmingly so.

The Sultan's guards became her guards, and all of the duties of the Sultan became hers. The Viziers committed a great deal of the city's well-being into her hands, and Dunya was torn: on the one hand, she was glad of the responsibility, glad to keep her mind occupied and away from the terrible memories of the Sultan's final moments. On the other hand, she was crowned less than an hour before she started to miss her freedom.

Her every moment of wakefulness was watched and given over to the people of the court and Palace, the matters of state and war, commerce and minting. Only in Dunya's dreams could she return, wandering, to the streets of Al-Rayyan.

Munir returned to the border camp, but he made it clear to Dunya that he would only be settling his affairs, and nominating a new Captain there, before returning to AlRayyan, to stay.

Upalu remained with Dunya, a flame of familiarity in a new and confusing landscape. The djinn had the freedom of the city, because Dunya had created a new position for her: Vizier of Magical People. All the concerns and needs of the city's djinni, ifrits, and other spirits, Upalu brought to the Sultana, with an opinion of her own and trust in Dunya, which she often expressed.

The day came, two months after Dunya's coronation, when merfolk were sighted in the river again, traveling north. The vineyards flourished and the people lived in peace. The sickness that had taken over Al-Rayyan was passing, healing.

After three months as Sultana, Dunya granted herself one luxury, one wish. She did not request it of Upalu, but rather, of her Viziers.

"I wish to take a leave of absence," she told them. "One day, and I will return to the city. There is a visit I need to pay."

"A visit to where?" asked Upalu.

"A place I've never been," Dunya replied.

The next day, Dunya dressed simply, took her mare—a gift from the Vizier of Transport— and rode to the south of the city walls. She had an escort lead her to a certain vineyard outside of the city walls. She dismounted when she approached the land and walked reverently on foot, as if she approached holy ground. She met the groundskeeper, and said, "Rashida was my mother. I understand I have some claim to this land."

The keepers of the plot welcomed her, and she lingered there for the day, thinking that this would be a wonderful place to bring the two little boys.

It was sunset, and she was just finishing a cup of watered wine, when she felt a shiver pass up her spine unexpectedly. She put down the empty cup, looked around, and saw a tall woman, dressed in all black, standing in the doorway.

"Hello, Zahra," said Dunya.

Zahra moved into the room. Snowflakes spiraled off of her veils as she moved them aside. "Hello."

"It is lovely to see you. I did not think we would meet again."

"Oh, little sister, you should not have lost faith." Zahra answered, sitting closer to the brazier. "It is lovely to see you, too."

Dunya thought of all the questions she had, and how many of them were not exactly fitting questions for a mere mortal to ask. But she did have one. "Are you really the Angel of Death?"

Zahra smiled. "I am an Angel of Death. There are many.

The world is wide, after all."

"You've really been watching over me since I was born?"

"Since the day I took your mother away."

After hesitating, Dunya asked, "Do you know what my mother meant, when she named me Dunya?"

Zahra's smile faded. "The world is a complicated place. It is a complicated name. I hope you know that your mother loved you very much. She was also wise for her age. She knew that you might not travel far. That your world would be restricted to the men you would marry, and the sons you would bear. But she hoped that, despite the place you were given, your heart and your mind would expand to welcome all, and to be as rich as the world."

Dunya did not trust herself to speak. "Thank you," she said finally. Then another thought struck her, and she sat up. "Are you here to take me?"

"No," said Zahra. She reached forward and touched Dunya's hand with two cold fingers. "I am only here to say goodbye for now. As a moment of grace."

"You were a good friend," Dunya said.

Zahra smiled at her. "Remember that, when your time comes. And now, little sister, we will meet again."

She vanished. "Peace go with you," Dunya said to the empty air.

Perhaps it was not so empty. The vines stirred on their trellises. The wind picked up. Dunya knew it was time to go home.

Nothing deterred her on her way to the Palace. She took a good look at the city as she passed through it. She wished the djinni that she met a good hearth, and she waved to the mermaids that she saw in the canals. She gave money to beggars and thanked storytellers for their words. She led her horse to the stables, watered her and brushed her down. Unhurried, Dunya prepared herself, and when she was ready, she went to the Lotus Gardens.

There, the nursemaids waited with the two little princes —or rather, Sultan Almas and his little brother. Dunya played with them while the sun went down, and after a while Upalu joined her. Munir arrived, fresh from the border camp, when the last sunlight had disappeared.

Dunya held Almas on her lap and smiled up at the stars.

"What are you thinking?" Upalu asked her. Munir leaned in for the answer.

"I'm thinking of a story," Dunya replied. Upalu raised an eyebrow, and Dunya added, "It's an idea of a tale, nothing solid yet. But I need help to tell it properly, and happily." "I'm good at help," Upalu said.

"Anything you need," Munir added.

Dunya smiled at them. "It's my story. And you're going to share it with me."

In the Kingdom of Al-Rayyan, the reign of Sultana Dunyazhade was an era of peace and learning. Dunyazhade lived and worked hard as a kind Sultana and a loving stepmother. As time went by, she grew famous not only for listening to all people, but for telling wonderful stories. She remained modest about her stories and her ability to tell them, always giving credit to a sister no one had met, whom she called Zahra-zhade.

Long after Dunyazhade passed away, the name Zahrazhade, warped by time into Scheherazade, clung to people's lips and memories, and the stories lingered on the wind. In time, Scheherazade's name and memory eclipsed Dunya's as the sun outshines the moon. But perhaps Dunya would not have minded that.

About the Author

Catherine Faris King is a Los Angeles based writer who studied English with an Emphasis in Creative Writing at Whittier College, and French Literature at the Sorbonne, in Paris.

The Ninety-Ninth Bride was originally published by The Book Smugglers in 2018. In 2022, Catherine F. King decided to self-publish with Ingram Spark. She would like to convey her heartfelt thanks to her family, especially her mother and father, and to her friends, for the constant encouragement and love.